MORE THAN A KISS

Fairy Tales And Curses

LACEY CARTER ANDERSEN   **ALEXIS TAYLOR**

BETH HENDRIX   **JENÉE ROBINSON**   **K.A. MORSE**

Rinna.
I ♡ ups
thank ups
for all your
support. means
the world to
me.
♡· KeeM

BEAUTY WITH A BITE

By Lacey Carter Andersen

Heat Level- Melt Your Panties- HOT

To my readers—thanks for always being so wonderful.
You have no idea how much I appreciate it!

~ Lacey Carter Andersen

WANT MORE FROM LACEY CARTER ANDERSEN?

Sign up for exclusive first looks at my hot new releases, exclusives, and contests from Lacey Carter Andersen!

Want to be part of the writing process? Maybe even get a taste of my sense of humor? Teasers for my new releases? And more? Join Lacey's Realm on Facebook!

This is not your classic tale of Sleeping Beauty. There's blood, death, and lots of sex! So... don't say I didn't warn you.

CHAPTER ONE

Beauty

I'm wearing the most expensive dress my parents have ever had fashioned. It's long, red, and cut low in the front. Normally, I'd love it, but not tonight.

Because tonight I'm being sold.

This dress is not for me. It's for the men who will bid to possess me. Just the thought of it turns my stomach and makes my palms sweat. I'm not a *thing* to be owned.

And yet, I will be.

My stepmother comes up the stairs, her every movement filled with rage. Her anger is so powerful that it cuts through the fog of her innocent appearance. She fools many men, including my father, into believing she isn't danger-ous. She appears as a golden-haired angel wearing a strangely youthful pastel blue gown, but she is much more than that. She is a puppet master, and all men are her puppets.

She turns in my direction, and I stiffen, preparing myself for the inevitable.

"Beauty." She says my name the way she always does, like it's ironic, like I'm some ugly creature named Beauty as a joke to all. Secretly, I think she believes that if she says my name like this enough, that's exactly what I'll become.

She forgets that she's only been a cloud over my life for the last eight years. Before that, I had thirteen years of being spoken to as if I *mattered*. I remembered how my mother would say my name, even when she was dying, like I was her whole heart.

Some things you never forget.

"Beauty," she says again as her gaze crawls over my body. "What are you doing skulking here? We're all waiting for you!"

"I don't want to do this," I say, holding her gaze.

She strides toward me and grabs my arm in a painful grip. "I know you always believed that you'd become one of us on your twenty-first birthday, that you would become a vampire of worth and that all your father's wealth and properties would become yours." Her smile is cruel as she gazes down at me. "But you didn't take after your magnificent father. You took after your human mother. And you know what that means—you inherit nothing. You are nothing but a burden to your father and your people. So, today you will do what is expected of you, which is to make yourself useful in the only way you can. You will become the blood-wife to a vampire, just like we discussed. If you don't make a good impression, instead of becoming the blood-wife to a wealthy lord of worth, you will become a thing... suckled upon by some moderately wealthy old man who will do things to you that you cannot even imagine."

Unfortunately, I can imagine it. I can imagine it so well that I feel a clammy hand closing around my throat. The faces of a dozen of my father's creepy friends flash in my mind. I start to gag, and grab my mouth, willing my lunch to stay down.

"Do *not* throw up!" she commands.

I swallow down the bile that's risen in the back of my throat and look toward the window. I could still run. I could—

"You won't make it," she says, amusement in her voice. "The second you failed to Turn, you became a prisoner in our home. The many, many Undead that guard over these lands will simply find you and drag you back."

She's right. The human cities are a good thirty miles from where I am. If I tried to run, they'd find me before I reached any place I could even hope to escape in. I already tried to steal a car, but the vehicles were guarded well, and I hadn't stood a chance.

"Beauty… the truth is that I don't care what happens to you. You've been a thorn in my side since the day I married your father. The fact that now my son will inherit your father's lands, well, that's all I ever hoped for. But your father will sleep more peacefully knowing that you were sold to a man of worth. So, suck it up, Beauty. Face your fears. For your father."

For the man who has agreed to this.

I loved my father, but the minute he forced me into this old ritual, I lost faith in him. Our relationship was broken in a way that we'll never heal from.

Not that I'll see him much after tonight.

My stepmother's grip tightens as she tugs me toward the stairs leading toward our ballroom. The Undead line this hall, animated because of the power of my family's blood. They wear armor over their pale green flesh, and their white eyes stare as if unseeing, but I know better. The Undead see all, and they can overpower even a vampire.

Despite all logic, my heart aches. On my twenty-first birthday they should've been mine to command. Mine to possess. Everything here should've been mine.

It's truly like I've been cursed.

When we reach the top of the stairs, my stepmother releases me. She smooths down the front of her gown and stares out at the massive ballroom.

"Don't embarrass us. If we have to, we'll drag you down."

With that, she starts down the stairs, not waiting to see if I'll follow.

I stand still, feeling vulnerable in a way I never have before. I'm not a virgin, not to the feel of man's teeth sinking deeply inside of me, or the feeling of a man's cock. But this is different… this is *wrong*.

But maybe they'll *be here.*

The hairs on the back of my neck stand on end. They won't be here. Other than their letters, I haven't heard from them in five long years. As half-breeds too, they despise other vampires. Yes, they rule their lands—triplets whose lands sealed them as rulers of a small manor and modest lands years ago—but that doesn't change their anger at the way the others treat them.

They won't be back tonight or any other night, so better buck up and paint a smile on. As much as I hated my stepmother, she was right. I couldn't escape this, but I could try to ensure my situation wasn't too awful.

I take a deep breath, grasp one side of my skirt, and start down the stairs. With each step, I can feel more and more eyes on me, like an unwelcome caress. By the time I reach the bottom of the stairs, the conversation in the room has died down.

Reluctantly, I raise my gaze.

I stiffen in shock as I realize that nearly every North American clan is represented and most of the clan members turned out. I see the younger men who rule their family's lands, but also the older, childless lords. My heart races. All the men stare, their unabashed hunger making my queasiness return.

Don't puke, Beauty.

I continue forward. Men smile as they take my hand. They lean down and kiss the back of my hand like I'm a lady they're courting instead of a blood-slave they plan to bid on.

With a forced smile, stiff words, and shaking legs, I slowly make my way to my chair beside my father. He avoids my gaze as I sink into the seat beside him. He starts to rise, to begin the auction for my life.

I look up to the stairs, to my untouchable freedom, and my gaze connects with intense green eyes. The air rushes out of my chest. The possessiveness of those eyes is like nothing I've seen in my life. The man they belong to? He's tall, broad, and muscular. A short beard almost manages to hide the strong lines of his face, but gives a dangerous allure that has everything inside of me tensing.

Two men flank him. I tear my gaze from him and find a man with light blond hair at his side, pale blue eyes, and supermodel good looks. He wears classically tailored clothes, and I imagine he never has a hair out of place. He stares at me with something I don't understand, a familiarity.

At last, I look to the third man. He's taller than the other two, with messy brown hair, brown eyes, and a smug face. It's as if he knows that he's beautiful, and he drinks in the attention.

Immediately, I recognize him. *Andrew?*

My gaze narrows, and I look back at the auburn-haired man with the beard, the man I thought was a stranger at first. Joshua has changed so much, I don't think I'd recognize him beneath his beard if not for those green eyes... ones I remember staring into far too many times.

The blond man, he can only be Kyle. He's just as beautiful as he's always been, but he looks like a man instead of a boy.

The years have been good to these three. I can see that

staying away from us was what was best for them. *So what brought them here tonight?*

"What the fuck are they doing here?" My father hisses, and I realize he's speaking about the Blackwater brothers.

My stepmother pats his arm. "Not to worry. They can't afford her."

Afford me? They couldn't possibly be here to try to buy me. Can they?

My heart races. *Why else would they be here?*

Beside me, my father draws himself up taller. The brothers move down the stairs, walking past the people who whisper at their backs but don't approach them. They move to stand in front of the other men, and just before my father.

Suddenly, it's hard to breathe. I think of the kisses we shared under the stars, and the letters we've penned to each other over the years. What I had with these men was special to me. And now... now they're going to see me sold to another man.

Because my stepmother is right, there's no way they can afford to bid on me.

And I hate that my treacherous heart is destroyed by the thought.

CHAPTER TWO

Joshua

I can't take my eyes off Beauty. Over the years, she's grown to be even lovelier than the girl I fell in love with long ago. Her long brown hair falls down her shoulders in waves that my hands itch to touch. Even from a distance, I can see how tall she is. And that she still has the face of a seductive angel.

But then there's her body—I bite down on a groan. Her curves beg to be touched. The low neckline of her gown is almost criminal, displaying the creamy skin of her flesh for all to see.

Anger and arousal cause my fangs to lengthen. Beauty is mine. She belongs to no one but my brothers and me. We determined it years before. We had thought that when she gained possession of her lands and Undead army, she could choose us as her own. Every day since we realized she was the one for us, we have worked to be worthy of her.

Never could we have expected this… our Beauty being sold off as a blood-whore.

It sickens me. Everything inside me screams in rage.

When I'd learned that she would be auctioned off, I'd

smashed everything in my room. I pounded everything within sight until my hands flowed with blood. Then, and only then, a cold knowledge had flowed through me.

We would buy her, and she would be ours forever, to hold and to protect.

Her father's gaze collides with mine. I can see it in his eyes—the same rage I'd seen the night he'd caught us kissing and commanded us never to return to his home, on penalty of death. He hated me, and he hated the mixed blood running through my veins.

More than anything, he hated that I reminded him of his own mistake in falling in love with a human. He might be able to force everyone around him to treat his mixed-breed child with respect, but seeing how much our own people despised us made him have to face the truth, that his child was seen the same way.

How could that man, the one who treasured his daughter too much to allow her to get mixed up with us, allow her to be auctioned off like this? He had options. What had driven him to this one?

"Welcome, gentlemen!" He says, barely raising his voice.

The room grows silent.

"We all know why we're here. My—my Beauty—has come of age and as you know, she failed to Turn. And so, we must accept her place in our community." He freezes, and for a second I think he might not be able to force the words out. "She will be a blood-wife to one of you gentleman, the one who wins her tonight."

Everyone claps enthusiastically, and he sits on his throne. Maybe they didn't notice the slight pallor to his skin, but I did.

Fucking coward.

His wife rises and the bidding begins.

My gaze sweeps back to Beauty. She sits like a queen with

her head held high. Her gaze is cold and emotionless, but I know her too well. She's terrified. That's why her gaze lacks its usual warmth, why she isn't smiling and laughing. She's buried her emotions and fears deep down inside. She sits beside her stepmother like an ice queen.

Our Beauty is too warm and kind to allow her heart to turn to ice. *When she knows she's safe with us again, she'll show us her true self once more.*

The bidding increases higher and higher. Men grumble and move back, allowing the active bidders to continue. I can sense the anger of our peers. They wonder why we stand in front. Why we haven't offer a single number, but soon they'll see.

Two men continue, back and forth. My gaze sweeps from Beauty to them. The bastards were old, childless vampires. One had already over-fed on three blood-wives, killing them without thought. I had heard the rumors that the other had a fondness for breaking beautiful things. These are the only men willing to bid a fair price for her, because despite how lovely she is, they see her human-half as a disadvantage.

But soon every vampire in this room will learn the truth—that we half-breeds are far more dangerous than they could *ever* imagine.

The two men continue to bid, and with each second our woman grows paler. It must have hit her that these two are her only options now. I can't imagine the terror she must be feeling about her future.

Don't worry, Beauty. They will never touch you.

The murderous old man scoffs and steps back, his face twisted in irritation.

The brute grins and opens his mouth.

"A million," I say, my words ringing clearly through the room.

All eyes turn to me.

For one second my resolve wavers, I'm the eldest by mere seconds. But even so, my brothers look to me for guidance. I was the one who decided we had to come here tonight. If anything should happen to them, it will be on *my* conscious for the short time before we die.

I glance at Beauty, and the moment vanishes. We all knew the risk of coming here tonight, but we also knew the reward. *True love.*

"That's—" her stepmother begins, and I know what she wants to say, that my bid is more than we can afford.

I challenge her with my gaze. *Say it, you witch.*

The brute's chest flares out. He didn't want me to outbid him, but he wouldn't spend that much on something he only wants to break, even if it kills his pride to lose to us.

"Sold, to the Darkwater brothers," her father says, and there's something in his tone that I don't expect—shock, not anger.

A few awkward claps ring through the room.

"But, of course," Beauty's stepmother continues, "payment will be due tonight."

I force a smile. "Of course."

But that's the thing. We'd determined we'd win Beauty tonight at any cost... but we never had a chance at actually *winning* her. She would've never gone for an amount we could afford.

So while we intended on winning her at any cost, we'd always known we wouldn't be playing fair. I want to feel bad about it, to feel this as a blow to my honor, but I can't. Beauty's gaze is locked onto us in relief, and honor means nothing. We'd give up anything for her. Even our honor.

I glance at my brothers. They give the slightest nod.

It's now or never.

CHAPTER THREE

Kyle

I close my eyes and send a command to one of our Undeads. He appears at the top of the stairs and moves down them, his steps awkward and clunky like all Undeads. In his hand is the briefcase containing every penny we could gather—all three hundred thousand.

As the men watch our Undead approaching, I feel the tension in the air. They don't believe we have the money. Unfortunately for us, they're right.

But we have a plan. It's a stupid gamble based on a fairy tale, but it's a plan all the same.

Turning, I don't mean to catch Beauty's gaze, but I do. Unable to help myself, I take the first step up the dais leading to her. Her stunning brown eyes widen in surprise, and her hand extends as if instinctually.

I take her hand, and the instant I do I feel a tingle move between us. It's hard to breathe, hard to think as I lean down and brush a kiss on the back of her hand.

It's impossible, unbelievable that this beautiful woman could ever be ours. I've thought of her every day since we were forbidden to see her again.

"I missed you," she says, so softly that I'm not sure if anyone other than her father and I can hear.

I smile and force myself to release her hand. There are so many things I want to say, but my words are meant for a private moment, not as a public declaration.

Looking back at my brothers, I realize just how close our Undead is to delivering the suitcase. Joshua nods, and we begin to whisper the words to the spell. The familiar words tangle through us, racing within our blood. I can sense the power building in my brothers. I can sense it growing, expanding out around us.

Our Undead hands the suitcase to Beauty's stepmother. The volume of our spell grows. I sense gazes on us. A room full of warlocks would be scared right now, but these vampires have no idea what our mixed blood is capable of.

My eyes connect with Beauty's. She frowns. I know she can hear our whispers. I know she can sense that something's off.

Trust us, I will my expression to say to her.

Her hands grip the arms on her chair, and I almost trip over my spell as I watch her rapidly rising and falling chest. That gown... I can't decide what I want more, to touch her like that lucky material touches her, or to rip it from her body.

"This isn't enough!" Her stepmother slams the case closed, drawing my attention away.

Her father rises. "I should have expected treachery from—"

We don't stop speaking. Our powers grow stronger and stronger, and then it's time. It's time to unleash our magic and see if tonight we walk away with our Beauty.

Or if we die.

CHAPTER FOUR

Andrew

*T*he spell explodes around us, cloaking the room in a golden light. I stagger, feeling that miserable sensation that always comes with using our warlock abilities —like someone's pulling my intestines out and dangling them in front of me.

And then, the sensation eases.

My eyes open, and I look around the room. Everyone is staring at us. Their expressions blank.

My heart races. It didn't work. *Oh fuck, it didn't work!*

Everyone falls at once, collapsing onto the floor. The three of us stand in the middle of them, our backs to each other, looking out at each person. The sleep spell… it actually worked!

"Told you." I can't help but smirk.

"For once I'm glad," Kyle says, bumping my shoulder lightly.

Joshua says nothing, he simply moves about the room, kicking at the people, making absolutely certain that the spell worked. *Always the leader. Always the cautious one.*

I, on the hand, turn to our Beauty. *To what's important.*

She's slumped over in her chair, looking even more beautiful in her sleep.

Only, she's more like a stunning painting rather than the woman who claims our hearts. A sleeping Beauty doesn't laugh, making those little crinkles at the corners of her eyes. And she doesn't pout, her bottom lip sticking out when she doesn't get her way.

As I move closer to her, I instantly miss her. The *real* her.

I kneel down beside her and prepare to scoop her into my arms, when her eyes pop open.

Stiffening, I freeze. *We hoped this would happen. Tailoring the spell to affect vampires shouldn't work well on a half-breed.*

As long as the others stay sleeping.

"Andrew?" She asks, her voice breathless and intoxicating.

I nod.

She leans forward and presses her lips against mine.

Every bit of logic flies out the window. Our carefully laid plans—the ones to escape as quickly as possible—are gone. There's nothing but the feel of her lips on mine, nothing but her scent teasing my nostrils, flooding me with memories and desire.

My hand digs into the back of her hair. She moans against my lips, and one of her hands rests on my chest. I feel the urge to sink my cock and teeth into her at the same time, to claim her as mine and form a full-bond between us.

I don't care where we are. I don't care if danger lurks in every shadow. One of my hands moves to the slit of her dress, pushes it open wider, and slides up her leg and along her inner-thigh. When I reach her core, I nearly choke on my shock. She's not wearing underwear. Oh fuck, she's *not*.

Our kissing grows more desperate. She's like a wild crea-ture, her arms holding me tighter. I use one finger to trail along the line of her opening. I wonder if she'll be wet for me. I wonder how tightly her inner-muscles will hold my finger as I dip in and out of her.

And I'm fucking ready to find out.

"Andrew!"

I'm yanked back. Snarling, I turn to the man foolish enough to get in between me and my queen. Joshua's green eyes are intense, filled with both desire and fear. My anger calms. He wants her too. He liked watching me kiss her and touch her, but he's more logical than I am. He's always been that way. Andrew's the practical one, the clear thinker.

Me? I'm the idiot that fucks everything up. But I *can't* fuck this up.

I have to stop.

"Okay," I tell him.

He gives the slightest nod and looks to Kyle. Both men hold themselves as if prepared for a fight.

We'll have plenty of time for our sweet woman when we're all safe.

I look down at Beauty. Her lips are swollen and her expression is thoughtful as her fingertips graze her mouth.

Oh, if she liked that, I can't wait to see what she thinks when we get her home...

"You want to go with us? Or stay here?" I ask her.

Her gaze meets mine, and her hand drops. "Is that even really a choice?"

For a second I'm frozen. Her voice is soft and yet power-ful, like an instrument strummed in the silence, vibrating through the air like a force greater than anything that can be seen.

I'm pathetic. Because god damn it, I've missed her voice. I've missed how it makes me want to crumble to my knees and worship at her feet.

I shake my head, trying to clear my thoughts. *What does a worshipper tell his queen in a moment like this?* "Unlike this little auction, it's absolutely your choice whether you go with us right now or not."

Even without her fangs, Beauty is our queen. She will always decide what she wants. She will command us, and we will scramble to do her bidding, because that's what a queen like her deserves.

Joshua speaks from behind me. "And even though we're freeing you, we want to be clear that doesn't force you to choose us."

His words hurt all of us. Yes, we've risked everything to free her, but we know we're beneath her and that we don't deserve her. Although we've never stopped loving her, she might not feel the same about us.

We've discussed this possibility many times in the darkness of night. We've tried to prepare ourselves for it, but even so, this woman can destroy us with her answer.

She tilts her head, and a playful smile touches her lips. "I'm afraid that I chose you long ago, and fangs or not, you belong to me."

The three of us exchange grins and some of the tension in the room fades.

"Then, my queen, we need to go," Kyle says. "We have no idea how long this spell will continue to work. You're still in danger."

She gives a simple nod. "Then, we go!"

As quickly as possible, I scoop her into my arms.

A little gasp slips passed her lips. "Andrew! I can walk!"

I huff. "Our queen never needs to walk!"

This time she laughs, and her arms tighten around my neck.

We start up the steps, passed the slumped over Undead, no longer animated by her father's blood. We're halfway up the stairs when we hear a sound that makes the hairs on my body stand on end. An enraged howling. And then more howls join the first.

"Fucking werewolves?" Kyle asks, his tone horrified.

I look down at Beauty, who holds herself tensely in my arms. "Why are their werewolves so close?"

Her big, frightened eyes lock onto mine. "We've been at war with a neighboring pack. Our Undead guard the border and keep us safe."

"But now no one is guarding the border…" Kyle doesn't say that the pack is likely invading Beauty's family lands from every direction. When they find the vampires sleeping they'll tear them to pieces.

Joshua starts to climb the stairs once more. "Then, all the more reason to hurry, to get Beauty to safety."

I start to follow him, but Beauty shakes her head. "No! We can't just leave everyone to die!"

"We don't have a choice!" Joshua says, not slowing. "If we wake the vampires, they'll take you from us. You'll be beaten, broken, and die a shell of yourself. Your life is worth more to us than all of theirs combined."

"I can't," Beauty says, her voice soft and filled with regret.

My arms tighten around her. "Beauty…"

"Wake them up." Her voice has that tone I've missed. The stubborn one I find so damn sexy.

But it doesn't matter. "We can't. We don't know how to."

Suddenly, we hear glass crashing behind us. Turning, I see a werewolf has exploded through one of the windows in the ballroom.

Oh fuck!

We move faster up the stairs. We hear more glass breaking. Growls vibrate through the air. We reach the top of the stairs when the window in front of us suddenly explodes.

Three werewolves stand in front of us, their fur standing

on end. Their teeth clench together and drool sliding down the sides of their mouths.

All of us tense at once. We are ready to do whatever we must to protect Beauty.

Slowly, I lower her to her feet, and push her behind me. My hands curl into fists. The three of us can take on these three and clear a path to escape, but if the ones in the ballroom join the battle, we're screwed.

A werewolf leaps at me, and I hear Beauty scream.

My hands press on its shoulders, keeping it back so that its massive jaws can't close over my face. With the strength of a vampire, I shove it back. The beast's back hits the stone railing with a crack, and it slides to the stairs. A second later, it shakes itself and climbs unevenly to its feet.

I hear the growls and snarls of the werewolves attacking my brothers. The scent of blood fills the air, but I can't look to see if they need me. If I take my gaze from this predator for one second, I'm dead.

Behind me, I sense more werewolves coming, slowly, quietly.

My muscles tense.

They're surrounding us. Soon, they'll attack. Our blood will coat these stairs, and our lives will fade away. We don't have a chance against these numbers.

Glancing below us, I count twelve werewolves. How are there fucking twelve werewolves?

We can't survive this. But maybe Beauty can.

My gaze meets with her horrified one. I grasp her waist, and with all my might, I throw her over the two werewolves battling my brothers. She hits the center of the broken glass and sprawls across the floor. For one second, I'm frozen, staring at her with her red dress spread around her. The broken glass shines like diamonds scattered around her on the floor.

Please let her escape. Let her reach safety.

Her escape is clear. She can leave all of us behind and leave this cursed life.

Even though her life will no longer include us, all we ever needed was to know she was safe and happy. If she gets up. If she doesn't look back, she just might be.

And then, the werewolf leaps at me and all else but our battle fades away.

CHAPTER FIVE

Beauty

*T*he glass cuts into my palms and blood stains the floor around me. The pain breaks through my panic, and I feel something awaken within me, something I've never felt before.

Climbing unsteadily to my feet, my vision sways and grows cloudy. My men are fighting, surrounded by murderous creatures who hate my family because of a century's old feud.

I can't do anything to help them, not with my fragile human flesh.

My brain feels like it's boiling, filling with a fire that spreads and burns through my veins.

The growls of the werewolves fill the air and the air is tinged with the coppery-scent of blood. Below us, I see werewolves attacking the sleeping bodies of the vampires. None have reached my father yet, and I can't let them. It doesn't matter what it costs me, or that my human body is fragile and useless.

I take a step and hiss. My shoes are gone. And my bare

feet feel the glass slicing into my flesh so acutely that I hesitate.

Something's wrong with me. Really wrong with me.

My heated blood feels hotter and hotter. I grip my head, trying to find some relief from the pain.

I can feel my blood pounding in my ears, and sliding over my skin. And then, my jaw begins to ache. And the aching grows until a scream catches in my throat.

Opening my mouth, I try to let my pain tear free from my lips. But instead, I feel fangs descend. And everything changes in an instant. I hit the ground, and my blood grows icy cold. My wounds no longer hurt, and my body feels strange. I feel stronger, powerful beyond anything I imagine.

My tongue touches my fangs, and I smile.

Hundreds of bright lights fill my vision, and with a nudge I awaken them our Undead army. I command them to come to our aide, to free our lands of these intruders. Because now I rule these lands and them.

Standing, I crunch through the glass, no longer feeling the pain. My Undead soldiers rise from the stairs and launch into an attack. They pull the werewolves away from the Black-water Brothers and four soldiers rise from beside my father's throne and attack the werewolves who prey upon the sleeping vampires.

In seconds, more Undead flood the ballroom.

I start down the stairs, grip the neck of a werewolf attacking Joshua, and snap its neck, tossing it to the ground. He's busy with two others, his body covered in bloody bites, his gaze desperate.

Kicking out, I send another werewolf flying. Joshua finally manages to get a good grip on the remaining werewolf. He tosses the creature into a wall. The werewolf's body slides to the floor, unmoving.

Werewolves run for the windows to escape. I watch them run, sending my Undead after them with just a thought.

I feel strange, more like a creature of magic than a vampire. But then, I didn't know what it felt like to be a vampire until now.

"You were supposed to run," Joshua says, between pants.

I move to stand beneath this tall, sexy man. Standing on my tiptoes, I kiss him, tasting his blood as I do. My cold blood heats, but I push him back. Another two steps down the stairs takes me to Kyle, I grab his shirt and pull him close for another kiss.

When I release him, he swears and tries to pull me back. I step out of his reach.

Farther down the stairs, I simply brush my lips against Andrew's, ignoring his attempt to capture my lips once more.

"Later," I promise him.

"I'll hold you to it," he says, the desire in his voice like a hand slipping along my spine.

I walk through the ballroom. My red dress is too long in my bare feet, and it's strange to feel it trailing through blood as I do so. I step over my father's slumped form on the floor and sit in his throne chair.

Smiling out at the chaos, the vampiress within me purrs in satisfaction. This throne is mine. This house, all our houses and lands—it all belongs to me. My gaze connects with my three men.

They're mine too.

"Wake them up," I command.

Joshua steps forward, a proud warrior even covered in blood. "We can't."

I cock my head. "Then who can?"

The men exchange a glance. "We don't know. The spell— it was found in an old fairy tale. We weren't even sure it would work."

My mind spins for a moment before I remember the tale. "Shouldn't our kiss have awakened everyone?"

Kyle frowns. "Not necessarily. A spell this powerful would need energy stronger than that from a kiss."

I cross my legs slowly. "Would the three of you fucking me be enough?"

None of them answer for a long minute.

Andrews's lips twist into a cocky grin. "I'd be willing to give it a try."

I raise a brow. "Come on then. I am the blood heir to the most powerful clan in North America, and I claim you three as my own. So, now, do as I command. Come fuck your queen and wake these vampires. I want them off my lands."

The men move toward me slowly. I watch them, overcome by their strength and by how handsome they are. When they reach the end of the dais, I'm humming with a need for them.

So this is what it feels like to Turn for the first time. No wonder it's usually celebrated with an orgy. My thighs are damp with my desire, and I know I need more than one cock.

These three better be ready for a long night.

"Take off your clothes," I command them.

The three men exchange a look and then obey.

"Slowly," I tell them.

Fucking Joshua is the first to remove his shirt, and I'm satisfied to see delicious tattoos covering his torso. *I'm going to lick every inch of them, suck those hard nipples, and trace my hands along the muscles of his arms.* The image comes perfectly to my mind and suddenly I feel like I'm crawling out of my flesh.

"Stop," I tell them. "Come here," I gesture to Joshua.

He approaches without hesitation, a man ready to serve his queen. *As it should be with one as powerful as I am.*

"Kneel," I command.

He does so.

I push back my long skirts and spread my legs. Then,

wordlessly I pull him closer and press his lips against my core.

He reacts like a caged animal. His hands grip my thighs, spreading me wider. He begins to suck and lick, pressing himself deeper and deeper inside of me, tasting me as if I'm his favorite meal.

I groan and grab his hair, pulling him closer. Pleasure radiates from my core, spreading throughout my body, and setting my nerves on fire. A moan slips past my lips, and I feel him groan against my body. There's just something erotic about knowing an alpha is between your legs, licking your juices and exploring your folds.

I bounce him against me, remembering every moment we'd spent together. I remember his arrogance, the way he orders everyone around in his life. In his house, he is the eldest brother and ruler of his lands, but now that he's mine, I rule him.

And I will do it *well*.

"Continue," I tell Kyle and Andrew, my voice husky with need.

Kyle's expression is serious as he removes his shirt and pants. He watches the man between my thighs with a jealousy that turns me on. When he stands in his dark boxer-briefs, I raise a brow.

"Remove them."

His gaze narrows.

I bite my lip with my fangs, feeling the blood that runs down my chin. His gaze locks onto it, and he takes a step forward.

Shaking my head, I smile. "Take those off!"

He raises a brow, but reaches for them and yanks them down.

"Holy hell," I whisper.

Oh the gods have blessed this man. *Fucking hell*. He's so

large, so long and thick that he must have been crafted by a god. I see precum moisten his tip, and I want nothing more than to taste it.

My gaze moves up to his face, and I know that *he* knows how delicious his cock is.

"Come here," I order.

He moves up the stairs and stops just behind his brother.

"What do you want to do with that?" I ask him.

His gaze locks onto mine. "I want to feel your ass tightening around it as I fuck you."

Oh, I'm sure he does.

I gesture for him to come closer. He stops at my side, his dick so close I could lean over and suck it without the slightest effort, but I won't. *Not yet.*

Instead, I tug down my loose top to reveal my breasts.

I don't have to say a word. He collapses to his knees, and his mouth locks onto one nipple as his big, warm hand begins to play with the other one.

"Yes," I whisper.

Between my thighs, Joshua's tongue begins to flick my clit in the most delightful way imaginable.

With one hand tangled in each of my men's hair, I fight off the waves of pleasure moving through my body. My gaze goes to Andrew. He's in nothing but boxers, his delicious body revealed for my pleasure. His erection strains against the material of his clothes.

"Take it off," I tell him.

He obeys, standing before me with an impressive erection. A shudder moves through my body.

"Come here," I indicate.

He drops onto his knees at my other side. Pushing away Kyle's hand, he begins to suck my other nipple. I feel it then —our mutual arousal has clouded the air with a power greater than anything imaginable. I begin to ride Joshua's face. I shout, my inner muscles tightening as his fingers plunges in and out of me. My orgasm is close, so damn close. When Joshua sucks my clit, I'm lost.

Screaming my pleasure, I crash over the edge, my body shaking as waves explode over me. I never knew this was possible, pleasure so consuming it's almost destructive in its power.

The powerful moment has created a connection between me and my men. Power for creation instead of destruction.

It takes me several long moments to calm my racing heart. When I can breathe again, I release my men and lean back in my throne.

"Is anyone waking?" I ask, my eyelids heavy.

"No, my queen," Joshua murmurs.

I smile. "Good. Now stand."

They stand in front of me. And slowly, oh so slowly, I suck their dicks, one after another. My mouth cradles them, warming and torturing them. When I return to Joshua's dick, I let my teeth slide along his length.

He swears, his head thrown back. His face twists in ecstasy, and then I sink my teeth lightly into his shaft. This is not the first time I've tasted blood, but it's my first time drawing it with my own fangs. It's my first time as a vampire.

I've always heard all blood tastes different. I've never understood it until now. I release my teeth from Joshua and lick it all away as he struggles above me. Then, I take him deeply into my mouth, until his tip touches the back of my throat. And again, I let my teeth sink into him. His blood is delicious, manly and earthy as it fills my mouth. My inner-muscles are tightening like his dick is in my pussy, not my mouth, and my nipples are hard. Blood and cock has got to be the most satisfying combination in this world.

And then, he comes.

Oh fuck is that even better.

He's insane as he rides me, grabbing my hair, shuddering as my teeth continue to hold him in place. And when he's finished, I draw back and suck him clean.

When I turn to Kyle and Andrew, their eyes are locked on me and cum slides down their shafts.

I smile. I didn't even have to touch them to bring them to completion. These men are perfect for my bed.

"Are the people awake yet?" I ask, already knowing the answer.

My men turn.

Joshua's voice comes out husky and shaking. "Not yet."

I rise from my throne and let my gown drop to the floor. "Sit on my throne Joshua, and I'll sit on your cock."

He practically races to obey, slipping into the chair behind me and leaning back, spreading his legs and waiting.

I position myself over him, grab his massive shaft, and sink the head of his cock into my ass. He swears and thrashes behind me, but I refuse to slow. I want this man inside of me, and his job is to satisfy all my needs.

Then, I gesture to Andrew. He leaps up the stairs and grabs my hips as he maneuvers me so he can slip into my pussy. My inner-muscles protest at the sheer size of him, but I wrap my legs around his back and draw him fully inside of me.

Oh, I am in heaven. There has never been anything as satisfying as this, as perfect as two men inside of me.

Lifting a hand, I motion for Kyle to come closer. He moves to my side, and I take him into my mouth, drawing my fangs along his length as I do so.

Then, we begin to fuck. Like people desperate for release, for pleasure, desperate to claim each other as our own.

When I orgasm, I scream around Kyle's cock, riding these men like I own them. It's fast. It's powerful.

I bite gently into Kyle's cock when I'm done, and he

explodes in my mouth. His cum and blood taste sweet and salty, a combination better than my favorite snack.

When he's done, I release him, and he staggers onto his knees beside me.

Turning to Andrew, I pull him closer as he fucks my pussy hard. Not hesitating, I sink my teeth into his neck and taste him again. I'll never get sick of tasting him.

He explodes filling my channel with his seed, coating me in a way I find possessive and sexy as hell.

I pull my teeth from his neck and lick the two small wounds, then lean back and pull Joshua's head closer. When his neck is exposed before me, I bite him too.

He groans and begins to fuck my ass harder and faster. His masculine blood fills my mouth, and for one minute this man seems to consume me, and then he explodes in my ass. His entire body shuddering.

I release him and sigh in pleasure. I've never been this happy before.

Andrew pulls out of me and sinks before me. I notice the people in the room stirring.

Pulling Joshua's cock out of my ass, I stand and look out over the room. All the people awaken, staring around themselves in confusion. Stretching my mind out, I reach for my Undead. The wolves are gone from our lands, and they stand guard.

I command the household ones to return, and soundlessly they surround the room.

At last the confused people look to where I stand, naked and surrounded by my men, their blood spilling down my chin. The scent of their blood and cum fills the air.

I smile. "I have Turned, and now I'm the queen of these lands, as I was always meant to be."

Perhaps it's my imagination, but I swear I can smell their fear. They would be foolish not to fear me. My lands and

Undead are ten times that of their lands and armies combined.

Tonight they treated me like a blood-whore.

Tonight they drank and bid on my body.

"If you aren't gone from my lands in ten minutes time, I will have my Undead rip you apart piece by piece."

Their gazes move to the Undead that surround the room, and people begin to rise in a hurry.

But my stepmother moves to me instead, bowing her head before my throne. "Surely you won't kick us out. We're your family." She looks up and meets my unyielding gaze. "Think of your father."

And I do. My father was a good man to me. Until he decided that he couldn't wait to see if the rumors were true, that sometimes half-breeds take longer to Turn.

Until he decided that he would let his daughter be sold, and broken and abused.

"Our smallest holding is in a little town of no significance. I am told that it lacks the refinement of our other holdings. You and father may reside there, but never again think to contact me. Never again think you can use my kindness for your own benefit."

Her nose wrinkles. "You can't surely mean to—"

My father grabs her by the shoulders and hauls her to her feet, his expression thunderous. "Shut your mouth before we both end up dead!" Then, he bows his head to me and hauls her from the room.

The others are rushing out, but I look away from them. They no longer matter to me. Only my three men matter. My three consorts. I touch each of them gently. "You came for me, after all this time."

Joshua's brilliant green eyes darken. "You had to know it was always you. There was never anyone else for us."

Kyle tilts his head. "We could never have allowed you to be sold or hurt. You're ours to protect."

My heart races. "And now, you're mine to protect."

Andrew grins. "What exactly do we need to do in return for this protection?"

I pretend to think. "There will be a ceremony to announce our blood-bond. There will be rings we'll need to exchange. And then... then you should make sure that you're comfortable on your knees, because you'll be spending a lot of time in that position."

His grin widens. "I think we can handle that."

I try to hide my pleasure at his answer. "And have you ever been chained to a bed?"

Andrew raises a brow. "No, but I have a feeling I will be."

Finally, I do smile. "Then, we should all get along just fine."

I stand and walk across the floor, the marble covered in the blood of my enemies

"Clean this up," I order my Undead. "And then bring refreshments to my room."

The creatures launch into action.

Starting up the bloodied stairs, I feel strange. I'd never imagined I'd feel comfortable standing naked in a room full of people. I never imagined that I'd enjoy seeing my naked men kneel before me as an audience looked on to see my clear dominance of them, but I do.

I think I'm perfectly suited to being a vampire. *To being a queen.*

"You know we made a lot of enemies today," Joshua calls after me.

I turn to look back at my alpha. "Well, do you know any more fairy tales?"

He frowns.

But Kyle is the one to answer. "This whole sleeping beauty spell was a one time thing."

Before I can answer, Andrew cuts in. "But I *have* always wanted to try that frog prince spell, maybe some Rapunzel hair magic…"

I smile. "Well, I imagine it'll take a while for the vampires and wolves to lick their wounds and come up with a plan, so why don't we take some time up stairs. If you're good, maybe I'll let you try a few things on *me*."

My men leap to their feet and start up the stairs, which makes me smile. I've missed them for so long. I knew they were mine from the beginning, and now the future I always imagined for us is ours.

In that moment, I make a promise to myself. No matter what happens in the days to come, these men are mine to love and protect.

And I'll do it well. No matter how many bodies have to fall in my wake.

CHAPTER SIX

Ella

*S*omewhere in a shit-hole town in the middle of nowhere, three months later…

My anger boils as I scrub the soot from beside the fire. My apron is stained. My hair is a mess. And my life is ruined. All because of *Beauty*.

I despise her with every inch of my being. All she had to do was *not* Turn. If she'd just remained a human, I could've had her free from my life forever. I could have remained on the throne beside my husband, the most powerful queen in all the clans.

The kitchen door crashes open. "The lord and his wife want their tea!"

I glare up into the big face of the head maid, a woman I've also added to my list of people to kill. "They'll get it when they get it."

She marches up to me and kicks me hard in the stomach. I fall into the ashes in the fireplace, coughing as I try to draw in a breath.

Isn't it enough my husband took on a second wife to continue to afford the things he likes? Isn't it enough that he blames me for losing his daughter's love?

I have to be this ash-covered servant *too*?

"Start the fire, boil their water, and get your ass in gear. You know his beautiful, *young* wife doesn't like to be kept waiting."

I climb to a sitting position and sneer at her. "Do you have any idea who I once was? Do you have any idea—?"

She cuts me off. "It doesn't matter, because now all you are is a Cinder-Woman. And that's all you'll ever be."

As she leaves the room, I pile wood into the fire. That woman… she's going to regret everything she's done to me. Because in order to become a true queen once more, all I have to do is kill my husband's new wife. And *Beauty*.

I smile. *And how hard could such a thing really be?*

A NOTE FROM THE AUTHOR

If you enjoyed this book, please consider leaving a review. Your reviews help other readers find my work. They're also a great way for me to learn what my readers want to read more or less of. I have so many ideas for stories, that if one series isn't gaining a lot of interest, I'll move on to another one!

Thank you for reading this story from my heart,

~Lacey Carter Andersen

ALSO BY LACEY CARTER ANDERSEN

Mates of the Realms: Mortals

Renegade Hunter

Cursed Hunter

Betrayed Hunter

Mates of the Realms: Immortals

Rebel Lover

Rebel Lies

Rebel Loss

The Dragon Shifters' Last Hope

Stolen by Her Harem

Claimed by Her Harem

Treasured by Her Harem

Harem of the Shifter Queen

Sultry Fire

Sinful Ice

Saucy Mist

Alternative Futures

Nightmare Hunter

Deadly Dreams

Mortal Flames

Twisted Prophecies

An Icelius Reverse Harem

Her Alien Romance

Steamy Tale of Warriors and Rebels

Gladiators

Monsters And Gargoyles

Medusa's Destiny

Keto's Tale

ABOUT THE AUTHOR

Lacey Carter Andersen loves reading, writing, and drinking excessive amounts of coffee. She spends her days taking care of her husband, three kids, and three cats. But at night, everything changes! Her imagination runs wild with strong-willed characters, unique worlds, and exciting plots that she enthusiastically puts into stories.

Lacey has dozens of tales: science fiction romances, paranormal romances, short romances, reverse harem romances, and more. So, please feel free to dive into any of her worlds; she loves to have the company!

And you're welcome to reach out to her; she really enjoys hearing from her readers.

Want to contact her?

Email: mailto:laceycarterandersen@gmail.com

Join My Mailing List: www.eepurl.com/cVwDNP

Website: https://laceycarterandersen.net/

Facebook Page: http://www.facebook.com/Lacey-Carter-Andersen-1940678949483316/

HEART OF STONE

By Alexis Taylor & Beth Hendrix

Heat Level- Need A Cold Shower- HOT

First Edition April 2019

Edited by Kala Adams

OTHER BOOKS BY BETH HENDRIX

Demon Exchange Series

Hoodwinked

Rise of the Morphlings Series

Of Blood & Twisted Roots

Anthologies

Penance (Found in Apocalyptic Holidays)

Polymorphic Passion (Found in My Bloodiest Valentine)

OTHER BOOKS BY ALEXIS TAYLOR

Hell's Wrath

Waking the Demon Within

Anthologies

Terror (Found in My Bloodiest Valentine)

Thank you to everyone who has supported us. Thank you AC Wilds for your incredible support we love you. A special thank you to Lacey Carter Anderson for letting us be in this Anthology and for sharing your wisdom with us. Thank you to Kala, Laura, Peggy, and Caitlyn for your support and for putting up with our last minute additions.

Thank you to everyone who reads this.

Thank you, Beth, for being a bitch.

Thank you, Alexis, for eating all of the doughnuts.

PROLOGUE

Maddox

*H*e was dead. The King --my best friend, my father-- was gone. It didn't make sense... How could this have happened?

My father was an immortal; he should've been impossible to kill. Yet there he was, his headless body on the ground before me, blood splattered all over the walls around it. It felt like it had been hours since I walked into the gruesome scene in front of me when in actuality it had probably only been a few minutes.

Just hours ago we were in this very room, talking and laughing. It felt like a nightmare when, just a short time after, the guards came and said there had been an attack. I thought...I don't know what I thought. That father had been hurt maybe. But not this.

Never this.

The guards had left a few minutes ago to search the castle to see if they could find the person who had done this. I'd already sent another smaller group of guards to search our little city. If no culprit was found there, they would change into human-like clothes and step beyond the veil that cloaks us from the human world. A murderer could easily slip past our gates into the city that surrounds us, hoping to be hidden in the chaos of humanity. But everyone knows that gargoyles are superior hunters... the bastard won't stay hidden for long.

But for now, I'm left here, with so many questions, and so few answers. And the questions? They circle through my mind and my heart, eating away at me. How did someone enter our castle and not be seen? How was someone able to kill an immortal? And what was I going to do now?

I was pretty sure I was in shock.

Looking across the room, I could see where his head had fallen, severed from his shoulders. There was a pool of blood around his body, you could smell the sickly copper scent. What scared me the most was the look of shock frozen on my father's face. That was something that would forever haunt me.

A shiver rolled through me, making me realize just how cold it was. It seemed almost as if the warmth and happiness that used to fill this room had been taken along with my father. A place full of love and laughter had now been replaced with a feeling of emptiness and silence.

What do I do now? Possibilities ran through my brain, one after another, so fast that I could hardly keep up. I wasn't ready to rule, we were supposed to have centuries before I would take over. I was supposed to be learning about how to rule, and finding a mate. Because without a mate, you couldn't become king.

Yes, it's 2019, not medieval times, but our people were still stuck in the past when it came to tradition. A King without a Queen -- no, it was unheard of.

My mother had passed when she had given birth to me, my dad, Jackson Franco, had never so much as looked at another woman. I wanted that, but if I didn't find a mate soon then the Gargoyle kingdom would fall into shambles.

A shadow caught my eye, and I remembered I wasn't alone. My father's best friend, King Richard, was off to the side of the room on the phone. I never understood how he and my father got along as well as they did because there was just something about Richard that put me off. Even though we had never been close, I was still grateful that he was here and I wasn't alone.

I wiped away the tears that had fallen. The last thing I wanted to do was show him any signs of weakness. King Richard was a hard man and a firm ruler, just like my father. Qualities I suppose all kings should have. That I want to have and I didn't want him to see me as a child since I would be ruling the Gargoyles.

When our eyes met, the mage walked across the room, stopping beside me. His gaze went from my father's body back to me. "I am so sorry, Maddox. This must be such a shock for you."

"Thank you," I said, even though the words felt hollow.

He cleared his throat, and I tensed, waiting for whatever was next. "I took the liberty of calling Jaques and the council members. They will be here within the hour." He held out his hand, then opened his fingers to reveal the thick gold ring with the gargoyle crest on it. "Your dad's ring was over by the phone, he'd want you to have it. I'd recommend taking it now, before the vultures descend and try to claim everything."

Taking the ring from his hand, I silently slipped it onto my finger. Over my fucking dead body would anyone take this from me. It'd been passed down from king to king for generations, and I would be the next King. I owed it to my father now, whether I wore the crown yet or not.

No sooner had I put on the ring, that I knew something

was wrong. My vision started to blur, and everything began to spin.

"Well, that was much easier than I thought."

It took me a minute to make out his words. The tone of voice was different, not that of a harsh king, but the voice of someone dangerous.

"What are…you talking about?" My words came out slow and unsteady.

The smile that lit his face made my stomach turn. "Your father would be so disappointed that it was this easy to trick you. It's kinda pathetic really, but then, your dad was just as gullible. Not suspecting what I had planned until it was too late. Do you even realize yet what I have done… Of course not, gargoyles aren't known for being smart."

His laugh seemed to echo through me. Richard… he'd been the one to kill Father? I didn't understand. How could someone be this sadistic to someone he claimed to love?

"Why would you do this? He was supposed to be your friend." And then my surprise gave away to anger. "You won't get away with this! I swear on everything, that I will stop you!"

Richard smiled a sickly sweet smile. "You're so surprised, and yet you wouldn't be if you knew the story of how this came to be."

I reach for him and stumble. Looking down, I could see that my legs have started to turn to stone.

Panic hits me. I'm slowly turning into my gargoyle form! And I can't undo it! That means only one thing, this is powerful magic. Magic capable of locking me into my stone form.

There are only two occasions where we are locked in our stone form. One is when a Gargoyle becomes of age, we are forced to stay in stone form for the week of our birthday. The second is when we have committed a heinous crime. A

Gargoyle can be sentenced to live a number of years stuck in his stone form. This, however, is only done as a last resort before death. It was the worst kind of punishment and Richard knew this.

"Oh yes," he says, still smiling. "You can't hurt me. Not while wearing your father's ring, which I took the liberty of cursing after I removed it from his cold, dead finger. Can you feel it? I've been told that it's painful when a gargoyle becomes stuck in one form."

I try to shout for my guards, but my voice comes out no louder than a whisper.

My heart races, if I can keep him distracted, I can buy myself some time. Maybe enough for the guards to come. "You said there was a story?"

His eyes light up, "A story unlike any you've heard before." The excitement in his voice makes me sick.

I scoff, trying to sound casual, even while sweat beads down my forehead. "I sincerely doubt that."

And I see it in his eyes. The asshole wants to prove me wrong. Whatever this story is, I know it is going to be bad. Where the fuck were the guards?

"Fifty years ago today, there was a sweet little kingdom of trolls. King Deagan had just watched the birth of his first born and future heir, but little did he know a mere hour later they would all be dead. You see, I have always been superior to my friends. I had always felt that instead of Deagan being the King of the Trolls, Jacques being the Vampire King, and your father the ruler of the Gargoyles, I should be King to all; not just the mages. Those three sorry excuses for Kings were an embarrassment to the crown. So I came up with a plan to take it from them. Deagan, he was my first target. He would be the most difficult to conquer but being the most powerful mage on the planet comes with its advantages. No one is truly immortal, everyone has a weakness, and though it took time, I finally found the perfect spells to rid me of them all. I went to see Deagan, and very much the same way as your father, I tricked him into doing my bidding. He was so worried about his kingdom; disease was running rampant and hundreds were dying every week. When I told him my spell would cure everyone, he readily let me have access to his entire population. My spell wasn't really a spell but a curse, if you will. It spread throughout the kingdom in minutes. The best part of my plan was that there was no warning. No one had time to react and within ten minutes the entire Troll population had been wiped out."

Oh my god. How had no one seen this monster for what he was? I tried to scream out but words failed me. Whatever he had done to me, now made it impossible for me to talk. Richard looked up at me as if realizing this and just smiled before continuing his awful story.

"When I left the Castle, the sight was glorious. Blood flowed through the streets pouring from the bodies that littered the kingdom. It was beautiful and the kingdom was now mine for the taking. However, imagine my surprise when I am about to head home and I find a little crying baby, all alone hidden under his mother, the Queen of the Trolls, bloody body. Now, I could have just killed him and been done with it, but where would the fun be in that? So, I took him home and raised him as my own. Even naming this poor orphan after my fallen 'best friend'. It was pure genius. No one suspected the grieving friend was the one who murdered them all. Naturally, his Kingdom was given to the nearest ruler, which was me, and my land expanded, but I was far from done. I spent 50 long years planning the deaths of Damien and your father. I can't have you ruining my plans though, not when I am so close to taking what is rightfully mine. We can't have you warning Damien now, can we? He is the weakest of us all, but with enough warning, he could certainly put a dent in my plans. Oh well, enough dilly-dally-ing, I have a kingdom to take over and a friend to kill. You have five minutes until you are rendered to nothing more than a statue. However, I have been talking a while so who knows how much time you really have now." With that last chilling word, he left.

I was going to fucking kill that sick son of a bitch just as soon as I could move again. There was nothing worse than a gargoyle being stuck in his stone form. Being trapped, unable to move or shift was torture. We were aware of everything going on around us, but we couldn't move, talk or do anything.

I needed to warn the others before he gets to Damien, but how the hell am I going to get out of here? Oh, fuck! Deagan! What the fuck was I going to tell him? All our lives, he had served Roman, he had helped him and kept him safe. We had never treated him as just Roman's guard but this whole time he had been a fucking Prince--no wait, he would be King now. Richard, that fucking bastard, was going down for this.

How could a man murder his friend and keep his son as a trophy? When I get my hands on him, I'll show him just how powerful a man of stone can be. I dare anyone to get in my way. A sound behind me snapped me out of my rage-fuelled thoughts moments before the world fell into complete darkness.

CHAPTER ONE

Rory

I will not scream! I will not scream! I repeated over and over in my head as I waited for the next lash from the whip. Even though I knew that after about the tenth lash, I would scream regardless of how bad I didn't want to. The not knowing was the worst part, they never came back to back nor were they timed. So, no matter how much I prepared, I was always taken off guard when they finally hit.

I screamed out in agony as the whip split open my back sending shocks of pain all the way down to my toes. Blood was pouring down my back and coated my torn dress. And the loss of blood was starting to make me feel lightheaded.

Gritting my teeth, I focused on Richard, or the Mage King, as he demanded people call him. He was a cruel, controlling man who desired to be the main ruler of the Kingdom of Magicae.

And I hated him.

But the gods know I had every reason to.

The King and one of his many minions were sitting at the table in front of me having tea as if nothing else was going on. He never forgot about me though, even now his eyes connected with mine. Before nodding at the man behind me, who let the whip fly not even a second later.

"Look at her, even now she glares at us," Jeffery said, patting his mouth with his handkerchief. "Really, I don't know why you keep her around."

I glared at both of them, gritting my teeth. He keeps me around because he can't break me. And that knowledge drives him mad.

Everyone who can see me shakes their heads, wondering why I can't just keep hidden. But what can I say? That in my dreams their blood pools at my feet? That I want nothing more than to see this man dead?

No, I'd never say that. The others would never understand. They're able to bow their heads and pretend being a servant to this man isn't awful. But maybe that's because he doesn't go out of his way to drag them to his chamber at random, to torture them for hours on end as he does me.

I was just a lowly servant who kept my head down and did my duties, but that never stopped his wrath. Always trying to avoid him as best I could because each time he laid eyes on me, I was dragged to his chambers to be tortured for hours on end. I had been at the castle for as long as I could remember, yet I had no idea what it was that I had done to cause this reaction from him.

The only good that came from my torture was that they thought I was in too much pain to listen to the private talks that happened as I was whipped. However, most of the time the only thing that kept me conscious was the fact that I was privy to whatever the King was talking about.

And I was determined to find enough information to one day destroy this man.

"Now that we've taken care of Mason, we have to do something about his son. If you wish to be the Kingdom's one, true ruler, then we cannot let Prince Maddox become

King," the King's advisor Jeffrey mumbled out. He reminded me of a weasel, short and skinny with brown beady eyes and thin, almost non-existent lips. He was just as big of a fuck-face as the King.

"I've already taken care of the Prince, Jeffery. The gargoyles are defeated, even if they don't know it yet, and they won't until I'm ready to make my next move," the King replied confidently as his grey eyes made their way to the man holding the whip behind me, and then he nodded.

I heard the whip before I felt it, then screamed out in agony as it hit in the same spot as before. *Fuck!* It took a long minute for the pain to ease, and then I was back to panting, left with nothing but my thoughts.

They were all so fucking crooked it made me sick. The King and his minions had already taken so much of the king-dom. One of these days I would laugh as I tortured them all, and bathed in their blood as the last light of life faded from their eyes. It was one of the thoughts that kept me going, maybe it sounded fucked up, but they deserved it.

The King's son, Roman seemed like a good person, but he was blind to his father's ambitions and actions. It wasn't his fault though, Richard was charismatic and way too manipula-tive for his own good and had most people eating out of the palm of his hands.

The other Kings fell for his ways and turned to him for matters that should have been taken care of by themselves. Maybe because he had been king longest? I never understood why no one saw through him.

"We'll take them easily, just as we took the shifters and trolls. We are *so* close." Jeffery almost squealed in delight.

Fucking asshole! Talking about murdering and making slaves out of people as if it was nothing. What the fuck was wrong with them?

The next hit caused my vision to darken as I tried to hold

on, nothing good ever came from passing out in the King's presence. There were lots of things that had happened in this room that I had locked into the *do-not-open* box in my head which I avoided at all costs. But at least I was confident they didn't find me attractive as a woman. That left most of my pain to creative torture.

"Yes, we will." Then, he lifted a hand to the servant with the whip. "That's enough, Wesley. Go throw Rory back into her room. I have a job for you to do afterward."

His minion untied my hands from the chains that were hooked into the ceiling. I hit the floor hard enough to jar all my open, bleeding wounds.

I whimpered as Wesley threw me over his shoulder and made his way to my quarters under the stairs. My back throbbed with each step, but I gritted my teeth. If I started crying now, I'd never be able to stop, and I refused to let them see how bad these 'sessions' really hurt me.

Especially not when I could already feel my skin pulling and burning, which meant my flesh was already knitting back together.

I wasn't a mage or any supe that I knew of, but one thing that made me different was that I did heal faster than most. By tomorrow, most of my wounds would have healed to the point that they were just scratches. I guarded this secret as best as I could. Refusing to allow the Medical Mages to help heal me and by acting as if I was in pain. So far it had worked well.

It seemed like a secret better kept to myself.

Finally, we made it to my bedroom, if it could be called that. There was a small bed that had seen better days, a table in the corner that was covered in books, and a chest barely big enough for my measly belongings, but it was all mine. The floor was scuffed and dingy, and the walls looked as though they were drooping due to the wallpaper that was working its way down the wall slowly.

It was ugly as hell, but it was my own. The only sanctuary in this awful place that I had ever known.

I was jerked out of my thoughts by the pain of being thrown back first onto my bed. Even though I tried my damnedest to stay conscious, I lost the battle as my vision turned black. The last thing I saw was Wesley smiling as he headed out the door.

CHAPTER TWO

Rory

Fuck! Was the first thought that popped into my head as I slowly woke up from my pain induced slumber. My back was itching like crazy-fire, which was a sign that my body was slowly healing. Pulling myself up into a sitting position, I groaned as the skin on my back pulled.

I wished I could just lay back down and pretend that I didn't have anything else to get done today. Unfortunately, I didn't get half of my duties done before I was dragged into the King's chambers. *Fucking Bastards!* And the last thing I wanted was to get another beating for not finishing my duties, I would be beaten either way, but it was always so much worse when I was found not doing what I was supposed to.

"I don't know what to make of it, Roman."

I perked up at the sound of Deagan, the prince's best friend and bodyguard. This was how I kept my sanity, listening to the prince and his friend. Feeling like I had company in this lonely life, even though I was more a ghost than a companion.

And it didn't hurt that I liked the sound of their voices so much. They were deep, and soothing, almost like a caress. I wasn't sure why I had such a reaction to them, probably because I was lonely.

Scooting a couple of inches closer to the vent, I pressed my ear against it and listened. If I was going to live in a closet, at least I could hear things I'm not meant to through the vents.

"Why do you only feel the pain during the night?" Deagan continued. "This just doesn't make any sense. You're the Prince! You can't just go running about after some *feeling*."

I'm a little surprised. Deagan sounds like the Prince is being impractical. And his tone is almost... mocking. But why? Their relationship never ceased to confuse me. Deagan was the prince's guard, yet they acted more like I'd imagine siblings would.

"You think I don't know that? I have things I need to do, but I can't do it when I feel like this. It's like I'm being tortured! During the day it's as if there's a rope tied to my stomach, and it's trying to pull me in this unknown direction. Then, every night I'm in so much pain that I can't sleep more than a few minutes at a time. I have to know why." The tone in his voice held both desperation and finality. It made me ache to hug him, which was confusing in and of itself.

"So you're just going to leave?" I could tell Deagan wasn't happy about the fact that they were going to leave the castle, and it probably had something to do with the fact that King Richard never allowed anyone to leave.

"I have no choice. I have to figure out why this is happening to me."

Interesting, the Prince is going to be leaving the castle? This could be my opportunity to get the hell out of here. For the Prince to leave he would have to take down the wards that keep me and everyone else trapped in this hellhole. Plans began to form in my head.

"Fine, but we'll be smart about this. You need to call

Caine and get him to come with us. I'll start preparing the truck. We can leave at first light."

Vehicles. One of the many human inventions that made our lives easier… and just might make *my* life easier for once.

"Thank you," the Prince said, and his voice was filled with sincerity.

I could hear the smile in Deagan's voice. "You know even when you're being an idiot, I still have your back. Where you go I go."

With that last word, I heard the door to the Prince's room slam shut. But I barely noticed because I was already plotting what to do next.

I knew one thing was for certain, I would be in that truck in the morning. I had waited so long for something like this to happen. The only way to get out of this hell was to take down the wards, but only the King and apparently the Prince knew how to do that. When the King left the castle someone on the inside would always bring the wards back up, which means this was a once in a lifetime chance for me to get the fuck out of here.

It was crazy to me that the Kingdoms had adopted most of the technology that was in the human realm. When the first Kings had come about, they had gotten together and erected a shield that kept the humans from discovering us. For the longest time, they refused to have anything to do with the mortal realm. Until a while ago, a human had wandered into our realm bringing in his technology. Ever since we have kept up with all the new things that they had come out with. Me personally, I wanted one of those cell phone things.

Ugh, I need to get ready. I pull myself up out of bed and head to my chest, if you could call it that. It was a tiny wooden box that was as rickety as the rest of the room. The dress I had on now was covered in blood and I could feel the breeze as I walked.

Grabbing a pair of leggings, t-shirt, and some new underwear, I made my way to the servant bathroom. You would think that the whole castle would have full bathrooms, but no, the king felt like the servants weren't worthy of that. So all we had was a tiny room with a small brass tub with a brass shower head hanging from the ceiling in the middle of it.

Luckily, there was still running water, but it was never hot enough or stayed hot for long. It was going to suck, but I had to shower and then dress my wounds. Undressing, I stepped in and sucked in a breath through gritted teeth as the water hit the lash marks on my back. *Damnit! This was worse than the actual whipping.*

Washing as quickly as I could, I stepped out of the shower feeling a bit better. After drying off, I took the time to study my wounds. They were already healing, but they were still bleeding just not as badly and even though I didn't think I could get an infection, I didn't want to test the theory. Grabbing some gauze I had stolen, and kept a generous supply of, I wrapped it around the wounds on my back. Thankfully, I had found long strips that could go around my whole torso, or I wouldn't have been able to do it myself.

Putting on my clothes, I headed back into my room to the chest and pulled out a bag. I shoved the necessities in it before throwing it on the bed. Now it was time to steal some food from the kitchen.

Things were already starting to come together.

CHAPTER THREE

Roman

*D*eagan and I finished our dinner with our usual vigor. But our meal was tense, and I could feel his unspoken worries.

When I motioned for the servant to leave my study, I finally turned to him.

"I've been thinking about it, and you don't have to go with me."

He sat up straighter in his seat, and I already know what he's thinking. The human world is dangerous. There's no way in hell he'll let me go alone.

"You have lost your damn mind if you think I am going to let you travel to some unknown place without me. I told you I was going to help you, and I meant it," he said back to me, just as I knew he would.

He was my brother even if we didn't share blood. He was the one I relied on and the one who had never let me down. I knew I could trust him and that he wanted to be my friend, and not just because I was the Prince.

"If you're sure," I smiled. "I just wanted to give you another chance to change your mind."

He grinned back at me. "Sorry, you're stuck with me."

I pushed away from the table and rose. "I'll see you in the morning then, and get some sleep."

"You too."

When I stepped out into the hall and closed the door, some unnamed emotion lingered over me. I was excited to be leaving, but more than anything, I was finally going to get to the bottom of what was going on. I knew without a doubt that whoever was causing this pain would die. Making it to my room, I headed straight to bed so that I'd be able to sleep at least a little bit. I was out as soon as my head hit the pillow.

Way too soon, the pain woke me from a dreamless sleep. The feeling felt as if someone had their hand inside my stomach playing with my insides. Getting up, I tried to make as little noise as possible, but the pain was too much. Falling to my knees, I heard a scream echo through the room and realized that it was coming from me.

It's time for the potion.

A pounding came at the door. "Prince?"

"It's okay, Deagan," I said, clenching my teeth. "I'm fine. Just the pain again."

There was a pause. "I'm here if you need me."

He always is. Thank goodness.

But we both needed sleep tonight, luckily for me, I had an idea. A way to give us one break from our miserable nightly routine.

Yesterday, after a particularly bad night, I'd come to a realization. If none of my potions could stop my pain, then maybe I could knock myself out enough to not feel it.

I had no idea if it'd actually work, but right now I was desperate enough to try.

This better fucking work! I thought before downing the potion. Another sharp pain caused me to double over as it felt like someone was cutting my stomach to ribbons. Whoever I was connected to was being caused horrendous pain, pain that I was also having to bare.

Relief swept over me at the thought that tomorrow Deagan and I would be able to find out what was going on. I only had hopes that I would be able to help the person that was being tortured.

Walking towards the bed, my legs gave out and I hit the floor. *Damn, I thought I'd have time to make it to the bed.*

I had a moment of doubt before I felt myself starting to go fuzzy. The pain lessened, and I let the darkness pull me back under.

"What the fuck are you doing on the floor? Get up before your Dad sees you. You know what happened last time," Deagan hissed at me, jerking me out of the unconsciousness that the potion had left me in.

Opening my eyes, his face was literally an inch from mine. "What the fuck, Deagan?" I growled out, while swatting at him and pulling myself to my feet.

The pain had finally subsided and that thought scared me as it always did. I was always terrified that when it stopped they were unconscious or worse, dead.

It made me wonder what had happened to the person who had been in pain? What were they going through when morning came? What kind of torture were they being put through?

No one deserves to go through the kind of torture that this person had been forced to endure. My main goal was to help and get this person out of that situation. I wasn't sure how I knew that the pain was coming from another living person, but every part of my being told me it was.

"I took a potion to knock me out."

His anger fades. I don't have to say more. We both know why I'd take a potion to knock me out. He hears my screaming each night.

"You didn't have to put your magical ward up," he says, and the anger creeps back into his voice.

"Ward?" I frown at him.

A part of me must not be feeling safe, because that was the only time my room would lock me in. It was a spell I had found when the war had started, my room had sort of a mind of its own when I was helpless or vulnerable. It would go into lockdown, and wouldn't open up again until the threat had passed. It hadn't happened in over 15 years, so I had no idea why it'd happened last night.

"I have no idea why the room shut down. You know that I have no control over that now."

He nods curtly. "As long as it wasn't intentional."

For a minute I feel irritated, wasn't I the one screaming in pain, not him? But then I look at him, *really* look at him. His black wavy hair, that usually never had one hair out of place, was now disheveled. The dark circles under his eyes made it obvious that the ward being up had really bothered him. He was even wearing the same clothes that he had on last night. "You look like hell, did you sleep at all?"

"No, I didn't sleep. I was worried about you." He picks up the potion bottle off the floor and sets it on the table. "But at least we might finally have a solution after this trip."

Despite the fact that my muscles are sore and my headaches, I stand. Our trip. My way out of this situation, is the only thing keeping me going at the moment. "Speaking of which, is the truck ready? I want to leave as soon as possible."

CHAPTER FOUR

Rory

*S*neaking out of the castle turned out to be a lot easier than I thought it would be. It was still dark when I made my way out, and the castle had been deserted. The relief that I felt at that had been tremendous because all night I had tossed and turned, afraid that the King would somehow realize my plan and stop me. So every creak or noise I heard on the way had me jittery.

I felt a twinge in my back as I walked closer to my ticket of freedom. My wounds were still bleeding a little, but they would be all healed by tomorrow. I just needed to suck it up until I was out of here.

Even though I was terrified, there was a huge part of me that was excited. I was getting away from this hell hole, and I would finally see Roman and Deagan up close instead of from the shadows. We had lived together in the same castle my whole life, but they had never seen me. My only solace was the few times I had heard the Prince and his friend laughing and talking. For some reason, just the sound of their voices calmed me in the of worst times. I wished every day I could have someone in my life to do those small things with. Once I got my revenge, I could try to have a normal life outside the castle walls with the humans that the kingdoms tried to ignore.

The truck was at the back of the castle. A rush of excitement and nerves hit me and had me running towards it. I knew this was my only chance to be free, and I wouldn't mess it up.

Opening the back door of the extended cab truck, I noticed that there was a big enough gap for me to fit under the seats and not be seen. *Thank fuck, I wouldn't have to ride in the bed of the truck.* I hadn't been looking forward to having to bury myself under who knows what back there.

Throwing my backpack in first, I pulled myself in and shut the door before shoving myself under the seats. I moved my backpack to the bottom of my legs and tried my best to make sure that I couldn't be seen. The only sound in the air was the beating of my heart pounding so loudly I was sure that they'd be able to hear it when they got in.

I knew Roman didn't have enhanced hearing, but I wasn't sure if Deagan did. The King didn't want me learning anything about the supernatural community, which had never made any sense to me, but because of that, my knowledge on everything was very limited. The only knowledge that I had were things I had studied in secret from books or conversations I had overheard in the castle over the years. The one upside to being invisible to most was no one thought to watch what they said around me. They barely registered I was even there.

Voices from outside the truck alerted me that Roman and Deagan were here. As much as I couldn't wait to get away, a small part of me wanted to know what they were up to before I escaped because I felt as though I was flying blind. Why did the Prince have to sneak out like a teenager in the rom-com movies that I had watched in secret? It made no sense.

"We need to pick up Caine. Everything is ready though. Do you have any idea where we're going or are we just following the 'magical pull'?" Deagan couldn't have sounded more sarcastic if he'd tried.

I had to stop the laugh that almost burst out of me. It really said so much about their friendship that Roman didn't punish him for talking to the future King that way. I tried to ignore the feelings his voice caused, but damn, was it sexy. Over the years I only caught it in passing, but now I could hear him clearly. His voice oozed sensuality, so husky and deep my body tingled with each word. *What the hell was that about? How is a voice affecting me so much?*

"Stop being a dickhead!" Roman spoke harshly, but he sounded more hurt than angry.

The pain in his voice made me ache to just wrap my arms around him and help with whatever he was dealing with. Which was insane. We had never even talked, so I had no idea where these feelings were coming from.

I had been locked up my entire life. Sheltered from the world and the first time I'm near men my own age I act like this? It had only been a few minutes, who knew how long I would be stuck in this truck with them. What the hell was I going to do?

My panic was interrupted by the opening of the doors and the loud music blasting through the truck as Roman turned on the radio. Thank god, if I can't hear them then they can't affect me. My small moment of happiness was shattered when a ringing noise broke through the music. Immediately, the music grew quieter.

"It's him," Roman said.

Deagan laughed. "I bet he's pissed, but then again he's always pissed. So what's new there."

"Just answer it before he gets angrier. We actually need his help and it would be better for us all if he was just his normal asshole self versus the pissed off asshole."

I heard someone hit a button, and then an angry voice came over the speakers. "Where the fuck are you guys? You said you would be here at first light. Last I checked, that was happening at this very moment. You may not have many responsibilities yet Roman, but my father has high expectations of me. I can't be gone for long or he'll notice I've left, and trust me, none of us want to deal with the wrath of my father when he's angry."

Oh god, that voice was hypnotic. So smooth and deep...Fuck! I had to get ahold of myself. This must be the Vampire Prince Caine that they had talked about.

"Calm your tits, Caine! We're on our way. Did you take the potion that I made for you last month?" Roman asked.

"Yeah I did, I won't burst into flames when we leave, but get here quick. I don't want any of the human help to get up and see me leaving," Caine said sarcastically, once again making me want to giggle.

When the fuck did I start wanting to giggle?

Well, it would be an interesting trip while I attempted to keep my hormones calm. That will totally work, right?

CHAPTER FIVE

Caine

*T*hese fucking assholes are never on time! When will I learn and stop waiting on them like a damn girl in heat? Being up before the sunrise already set me in a bad mood, but now Tweedledee and Tweedledum were late. On top of that, the dipshit Maddox was ignoring me. One teeny argument that resulted in a few pigs being drained and boo hoo he went sulking to his room and refused to talk to me. Why I was friends with these dipshits, I would never know.

It'd been harder than I cared to admit to sneak out due to the fact that my sister, Ella, now always stays up to watch the sunrise. Roman had given her a potion to keep the sun from burning our skin. She's always been curious and sad that she couldn't go outside and feel the sun on her skin. My dad had tried to help and had even built her a garden in the castle with artificial sunlight, but it hadn't helped much. As annoying as I now found it to sneak out with her awake, it was nice to see her happy.

I heard the truck before I saw it and grabbed my bags. Fuckers had taken long enough to get here. I was going to pay for this trip, I just knew it. As soon as Dad finds out I am gone, there will be hell to pay.

Dad would have me stuck to his side like glue for years after this. Yeah, most people probably thought being princes meant that we could do whatever we wanted when we wanted, but how could they possibly know?

Everyone who looked at us saw the stereotype. Stupid spoiled princes. What they didn't see was how controlling our fathers were. We weren't allowed to leave the Kingdom without permission. Roman feeling some pull that caused him pain-- yeah, that wouldn't cut it. There would be no excuse they'd except for us taking off.

Once again, I found myself wondering why I did what I did for my friends. Maybe because you like them… a little. Even if they're always late and giant jackasses. The truck pulled up alongside me and I had to stop myself from killing them when I saw the stupid grins on their faces. I had been hiding out here forever, they should have left earlier. They knew it took three hours to get here from their stupid ass castle.

"You better wipe those stupid looks off your faces. This shit isn't funny. I do not have the time to sit around all day waiting on you two assholes." Laughter erupted from the truck as I made my way to the back. I chucked my bags in before taking my seat, still silently plotting the demise of my two best friends.

Roman's looks were not typical of a mage. He was over six feet tall with long hair that was like fire. His black eyes were intense, but he usually had a smile on his face. He was covered in mage ink, which increased his magic.

Deagan, on the other hand, was his almost complete opposite, I had never seen another troll, but I had to imagine that he was tall even for their standards. He towered over everyone and looked scary as hell with his black wavy hair and a black beard. It didn't help that he usually wore a scowl on his face unless he was with us. It was pretty much the only time I had ever seen him smile.

"Sorry, we had to make sure the castle was deserted. And you know Deagan, he had to make sure we had everything for any situation that may arise."

Roman was trying to act nonchalant, but even I could tell he was worried. So for that reason alone, I decided to stop bitching.

"Fine, let's get going. Despite being able to be out in the daytime thanks to that potion of yours, I have a healthy fear of the sun," I say.

Roman turns and looks back at me. "Probably not a bad idea, what with the whole bursting into flames thing."

"At least I don't accidentally turn people into barnyard animals!"

"Alright, alright," Deagan said. "Let's get going. We've got no telling how many hours before we get to wherever this pull is coming from, we might as well not drag it out."

Starting down the driveway from my manor, I watched the trees surrounding it as we passed. Our Castle was surrounded by a forest, which was smart since we were supposed to drink from animals and not humans or other supes.

As I started to relax, a new feeling came over me. Something... something was wrong.

I blamed my anger and frustration for my lack of awareness because the second I calmed down and took a big breath the smell hit me. The truck was full of the unmistakably, delicious aroma of blood. Now, this wasn't the usual smell that followed Deagan after his run-ins with King Richard, or Roman when he had been training. Their scents always changed when they were anxious, excited or frightened, but no, this smell was single-handedly the best scent I had ever smelled in my life. A delicious aroma mixed with a touch of soap, lilies, and fear. Despite how alluring the smell was, what worried me was it was coming from right beside me.

"Stop the fucking truck, right now," I said.

The truck stopped almost instantly. Throwing the door open, I leapt out of the truck before anyone could move. My gaze went to the spot beside me. No one was there, right? But my nose didn't lie. So, where could they be?

First I looked in the back of the truck, nothing there. Then, I ran my hands along the actual seat, wondering if someone was hidden with a spell, or if there was a hidden lever. It could have been anything, there were tons of known invisibility spells.

Finally, frowning, I crept down and looked under the seat, and instantly found what I was looking for. My face was inches from a pale white leg attached to a black boot.

"Shit," whispered a feminine voice, before I grabbed onto the leg and jerked whoever it was out of the truck.

Over the years our enemies had sent many people to kill us, but a female hiding in our truck had to be a first. Even if she clearly wasn't the smartest of assassins. One quick pull and the girl went flying out of the truck, landing with a huge thud on the ground. Ice blue eyes met mine, and I froze.

It was a woman, a small one, but a woman nonetheless. Her honey blonde hair was up in a bun atop her head. Bright blue eyes that looked a little to big for her face and a small nose that fit perfectly. Her mouth was small, but plump and pulled into a line.

She smelled amazing like chocolate and female, and I knew instantly that my eyes had turned red. She jerked as she looked at me. I was instantly curious about her.

CHAPTER SIX

Rory

I landed on the ground hard enough that my teeth slammed together. The man in front of me had a voice that didn't do him justice. *I thought vampires were supposed to be pale.* But not this one. Instead, the vampire with a sexy voice had tanned skin, bleach blond hair, and emerald green eyes-- eyes that were currently glaring at me as he frowned.

He sniffed the air and those gorgeous green eyes turned red. I couldn't help the jerk that went through my body as I noticed them. It couldn't mean anything good for them to change like that.

"You have got to be the worst assassin in the world. I could smell you from the moment I stepped into the truck."

"You think I'm an assassin?" *How could they possibly think that?*

He smirked. "Don't even try it, we're not that naive."

"But I'm not! I'm--"

"A beautiful woman? Yeah, but a little skinny for my taste. Even if I bet you taste like heaven," the vampire named Caine grinned, but his smile didn't quite reach his eyes.

Maybe I should be afraid. A vampire was saying he was

going to kill me, after all. But I'd always had too much atti-
tude for my own good.

"Of course I am skinny, you fuck face. I've been held
captive my whole life. It's not like they cared enough to feed
me well," I shouted. Fucking asshole. Who was he to call me
skinny?

Two doors slamming snapped me out of my rage-fuelled
fog. Roman and Deagan stood looking at me, both resem-
bling fish with their mouths wide open. They looked so
shocked it was almost funny. If their dickhead, bitch buddy
had not just insulted me I might have laughed.

"Who are you? How did you get in my truck?" Deagan
says, looking in my direction. "I checked it eight times to
make sure everything was safe for Roman. This is not good.
God, Ro I'm so sorry. I failed you! I honestly didn't think
some little girl would be hired to hurt you. Why didn't I
think someone could fit under the back seats of the truck?"

"It's okay," Roman said. "It's not important how she got
here, what's important is figuring out who she is and why
she was in my truck."

The vampire scoffed folding his arms in front of his chest.
"Clearly, she's a mortal sent to assassinate us."

"I'm not an assassin!" I say again.

Deagan draws his sword. "Talk faster."

My heart raced. "First off, I'm Rory and I've lived, if you
can call it that, in the castle with both of you for as long as I
can remember."

"No," Roman says, "we would have noticed you."

I laugh. "Yeah, because everyone notices quiet servants."

"Do you believe her?" the vampire asks Roman and
Deagan.

They hesitate, looking at me frowning.

"That still doesn't explain how and why you ended up in

our truck," Deagan presses, but he's not holding his sword as tightly.

"I climbed in right before you two did. If I didn't get away from Roman's asshole father, he would have beat me until I finally left this life. I literally walked out of the castle, and climbed in the back," I started before Deagan once again interrupted me.

"I don't believe you. Nobody knew that we were planning to leave. So how did you even know we were leaving." Deagan commanded, the damn troll was starting to piss me off.

"For the last time, I'm not an assassin! I am just a girl who refuses to be whipped and abused any longer. I heard you through the vents in my room. You were just my ride out of that shithole. But don't worry, you got me out. I don't need to stick around." Men were so infuriating, they were all staring at me as if I had grown a second head or something.

"There's no way," Roman stated.

"Well as fun as this has been, I'm out."Pulling myself off the ground, I grabbed my bag that had been thrown beside me and grimaced as I put it on my back. I gave a one-handed salute before turning and starting my walk down the road. *Could you be any lamer?*

"You, just wait a second! You can't say all of that and seriously expect us to let you just walk away, do you? My father would never do such things. How dare you accuse him!" Roman shouted, causing me to turn back towards them.

Deagan just stared at me with a knowing look. It seemed as though I was not the only toy the King had.

"Actually, I think she might be telling the truth."

I stared at Caine, surprised to hear him backing me up. But why?

The vampire sighed and ran his fingers through his blond hair. "Your dad has a bit of a reputation."

"What kind of reputation?"

"For being cruel. For hurting people. I heard..."

"What? Come on, Caine. I deserve to know the truth."

"I heard he beats and rapes his servants, I heard--"

Roman's fists bunched up. "That's my father!"

"You asked for the truth! I didn't want to tell you. Why the fuck would I? No one wants to know their dad is an asshole. I was even under a blood oath not to tell you. "

Roman looked from me to his vampire friend, then to Deagan. "Have you heard any stories about my father?"

Deagan looked away, but not before we all saw the sad look on his face.

Silence fell over us.

"Look," I said. "I didn't want to cause problems. I just wanted to tell you because I know you're friends with Prince Maddox, and your dad mentioned that he'd hurt him. I thought maybe that was why you felt that pull."

He stared at me. "When did you hear that? And how do you know about the pull?"

I shrugged. "I hear things... when your dad whips me."

"He whips you, why?"

"Probably because he is a sadistic bastard. Who knows?" My feelings for his father caused my voice to be hard.

My gaze swung to Roman. The mage looked enraged. Any six foot something man would be scary that angry, but he also had a dangerous edge to him. It wasn't just that every inch of his exposed skin was covered in black tattoos. It was his long red hair that looked like a flame and his already black eyes seemed to go even darker.

"Why in the fuck has no one mentioned this to me? I get why you didn't Caine, but Deagan if my father was hurting you, why didn't you tell me? I would have helped you." Roman closed his eyes, his fists clenched tightly.

I took a step back. It seemed I'd done what I planned to.

I'd told him the truth about his father. It was time for me to go before they started asking more questions. The sooner I could distance myself from them, the better.

I took another step backward. "Thanks again for the lift, but I think it's time for me to go."

Deagan's hand tightened on his sword as I turned to walk away. Old wounds at some of the King's torturous actions had me terrified. I was instantly transported back to my torture.

Taking off running, my body instantly rebelled as pain shot through my body. Being lost in the past, made me feel as though I would never get away if I didn't escape.

Arms circled me as I was pulled back against a strong chest. I couldn't help the scream that burst out of my mouth.

"You, little lady, aren't going anywhere. Now, you say -- and I believe you-- that King Richard tortured you. My question is why now? How is it you found yourself in the back of Deagan's truck?" Caine's silky voice was doing things it shouldn't to me. It was instantly calming, which I was so thankful for. *Who knew that I had triggers now that made me wanna run?* However, It also made me wonder if seduction was part of a Vampire's allure.

Before I could formulate a response I was pulled out of his warm arms and was suddenly face to face with the still enraged Mage Prince Roman.

"How have we never seen you? I know the people in my castle!" Roman half shouted at me.

But even though his words were angry, I wasn't afraid. Instead, I glued myself to Caine, his body hard, but soft at the same time as I leaned back against him.

What had he said?

Too bad I'd only half heard what he said. Ugh, what was it about these guys that made my body respond this way? I couldn't focus with them surrounding me like this.

"Are you guys fucking kidding me right now? Who cares about that. What matters is getting to Maddox if he is the one in need of help." Deagan took my hands so gently that it surprised me.

Looking up into his eyes, he looked devastated. At that moment, I would've given anything to take that look out of his eyes. His thumb ran circles over the back of my hand. His hands were so warm but rough. My stomach started doing flips the minute his hands had taken mine.

"What did you mean about Maddox? Do you really think the pain and pull Roman feels is from him?" Deagan asked, slowly as if he somehow knew I was having issues with keeping up with what they were saying.

I'd completely forgotten I'd even mentioned what I had overheard with everything that had happened. Deagan really must care about all the Princes if he paid that much attention to what I was saying.

Silence filled the air as all eyes were suddenly on me. All three men looked extremely worried. This pull Roman had mentioned must have been a big deal to cause this kind of reaction. I didn't particularly want to stay out in the open like this, so maybe I could use my information to get a little further away? Maybe to another town and as far out of the King's reach as I could get.

"I'll tell you everything I know if you will get me away from this hellhole."

I figured they'd talk it over, or maybe take a few minutes to think about it, but no sooner had the words left my mouth when Deagan pulled me towards the truck.

"Get in. We need to leave now. If the King is behind this then Maddox is in a lot of trouble. Roman, you're in the back with Caine. I want Rory upfront with me. I'm not sure if we can completely trust her yet, and I won't risk your safety on a hunch."

His mistrust of me hurt way more than I cared to admit, but I had to push that to the side if I wanted to get away. However, it really shocked me when no one put up a fight. For Deagan, not being a Prince, the others really respected his decisions.

"Thank you, while you're doing it for a different reason, I really didn't want to sit next to that dickhead," I said nonchalantly nodding my head towards Caine before jumping into the truck.

I heard an explosion of laughter behind me and for some strange reason knowing I had made those three big tough guys laugh pleased me. I'd just gotten buckled in when a small pouch was thrown at me from the back of the truck. Roman's voice was quiet as he spoke a weird language I had never heard. It came from right behind me and warmed every part of my body.

"Drink this, we can't have the smell of your blood intoxicating our Vampire, now can we? I would much rather keep you alive than watch you become his lunch. Numbnuts over here is practically drooling." Roman laughed as my head snapped up, looking back my eyes colliding with deep red ones.

"Actually apart from the stains on my clothes, I'm already healed and unless Mr. Snappy Pants wants to lose his balls, he will keep his fangs to himself. I ran away because I refused to be a punching bag, and I will not become someone's blood bag." I looked right at Caine as I spoke. Stupid Vampire was actually licking his lips.

Haha, he thinks he's scary, but scared is the last thing I am right now. Crossing my legs to try and hide my discomfort, I turned my attention back to the sexy Troll beside me. He didn't look how I imagined a troll would look. I mean, he had the height thing down. He must have been over seven feet tall. Long black wavy hair and a thick beard covered his face. He had that 'I just got out of bed' look. The clothes he wore looked as though they had been made just for him, tight and fitting in all the right places. You could see the outline of his chest and stomach muscles.

"If you don't want to be eaten in an entirely different sense, you need to stop whatever it is you are thinking while you look at him, right now. It's bad enough you smell so good without you being turned on too." Caine's red eyes speared me when I turned to look at him.

"I'm not thinking anything."

"Not about how hot he is?"

Shit. "Nope."

"And that delicious smell isn't your arousal?"

Fuck. "Nope."

I tried to keep my face blank to let him know that he wasn't affecting me, but holy hell it was as though his words had set me on fire and I had to squeeze my thighs together. Hopefully, that would keep him from smelling how turned on I was at the thought of his mouth on me.

"Also," Caine continued and I could feel his red eyes looking me over. "If you were beaten so badly, how are you already healed? You shouldn't even be able to move."

I know he had the right to be suspicious. I mean, I didn't understand it either. What would I tell him 'oh, I am human but within a day my injuries always magically heal?' No way. I had never told a soul about this, I couldn't start now. No matter how pretty they were. Caine was still talking and I struggled to contain my emotions and listen to what he was saying.

"You're mortal as far as I can tell but you're most definitely hiding something. A mere human shouldn't even know how to block me reading them. For a few minutes, you could. Care to explain?" Caine had leaned forward and grabbed my arm clearly to get my attention, but I heard nothing that he had just said. His eyes, that had been blood red a few moments ago, were now as black as the night sky. God, this man was beautiful and I hated it. To save myself some time, I made a show of drinking the pouchy thingy Roman had given me and to my surprise, he came to my rescue.

"Be nice Caine, she clearly finds Deagan fascinating. The poor girl can't keep her eyes off him. I mean think about it, wouldn't you be amazed? He is kind of impressive. All tall and muscly, not at all what a novice would envision a troll to look like. Add in the fact he is also one scary son of a bitch. You can't blame her for her thoughts."

"It's not nice to read minds. Trust me that my mind isn't a place that you want to be," I said the first thing that crossed my mind. *Wait a second, why did I say that?*

Realization hit me at that moment that the pouch Roman had given me was definitely not for healing, but had taken my filter away. *That mother fucker!*

"So, Rory, was it? Tell me, what do you know of us?"

I attempted to cover my mouth with my hand, but unfortunately, it didn't do much because you could still hear every word. "I could hear you both talking from my room under the stairs, I knew your names and that you felt this pain. I knew you were the Prince and Deagan was your friend. The rest I learned from the King. He hates Deagan, said all the time about how he loved the fact that he had the last Troll as a servant. I had heard him talking to the other Kings and that was how I learned of Maddox and Caine. The rest I managed to learn from the few books I had been able to steal from the cook."

"Are you afraid of Deagan or something?" Caine asked with a smirk on his face and I instantly wanted to smack it off.

"I wasn't staring at him because he is scary. He's just so hot. Well really the three of you are so insanely sexy, it's driving me insane. I have never even thought about sex or men, but since you found me all I have been thinking about is what you look like under those clothes. What Caine's fangs would feel like nibbling at my breasts or how much fun it would be to climb Deagan and wrap my legs around his waist." *Just kill me now, this was just ridiculous.* I tried to stop the words, however, it was like word vomit and I just couldn't keep myself from continuing. "Caine is kind of an asshole though, so I feel he would be very selfish in bed and not really worthy of my time. He would be kind of a bucket list thing, you know? Roman, however, you can tell just by looking at him that he's the fuck them hard and fast type. Everything about him screams 'in the moment'. While Deagan seems like he would take his time, and would be all about pleasing the woman first before he took his own plea-sure. He oozes control, and he would definitely be adven-turous and demanding. He strangely also seems the more romantic of you three. I have a question though, have any of you shared a girl before? I never heard either Roman or Deagan talk about women and believe me I heard them talk a lot. I know the King had worries that you both were actually much closer than anyone thought. So are you together or do you like girls?" A hand was suddenly around my mouth and Roman whispered something in my ear too quietly for me to hear.

"What the fuck did you do Roman? Are you trying to get the girl killed or fucked? I can't tell right now. Fuck!" Deagan's voice seemed to snap me out of a fog I had been in. I was so confused.

Yes, it was the truth but god, why did I tell them anything? It was as if I didn't have a filter. My cheeks flamed in embarrassment.

Before I could put much thought into it, Deagan was suddenly at my side of the truck. I had been so lost in thought that I didn't even realize the truck had stopped. The door flew open, and I was unbuckled and pulled from the truck before I could ask what was wrong. He didn't look mad, but his eyes were blazing.

Opening my mouth to ask what was going on, his mouth was on mine so fast I didn't even get the first word out. His hands, that had been on my hips, had found their way into my hair and he jerked me closer to him. There was nothing sweet about it as he pressed his whole body against me.

I was taken aback by how abrupt the kiss was, but I couldn't stop myself from responding. My body instantly going hot as I ran my hands up his sides to grip the back of his neck and keep him from getting away. I wasn't really sure what I was doing, but I followed his lead as he started to run his tongue over my lips before biting the lower one causing me to gasp.

The heat that started in my stomach slowly started to move lower as my center throbbed. I could feel his erection pressed against me, and it was just too much. We needed to be closer. With my grip on his neck, I pulled myself up and wrapped my legs around his waist. Aligning my core with his hard length caused us both to groan as he broke the kiss.

He started to trail kisses across my cheek, his beard tickling my ear before nibbling more kisses down my neck. One of his hands moved out of my hair and caressed its way under my shirt and to my bare breast. As soon as his fingertips got to my nipple, my body ignited in pleasure.

Holy hell, why had I never done this before? It was my last thought as Deagan was ripped away from me. Hands from behind caught me before I could fall to the ground. Turning around, I could see that Caine was the owner of those hands.

"What the hell are you thinking? We don't even know if she can be trusted," Roman spoke sharply before his flaming eyes landed on me.

I was furious. For the first time in my life, a man was giving me something other than pain, and Roman had just taken that from me. Pulling myself out of Caine's hands, I turned and not saying a word jumped back in the truck. Tears were falling down my face, I needed Deagan, and I had no idea why but every part of my body screamed for him, which only proceeded to confuse me even more. They were supposed to just be my fucking way out of the castle, I wasn't supposed to get involved with them.

Caine leaned into my open truck door. "You should ignore Roman, he's just jealous that Deagan had the balls to do what we all wanted to. It was one of the most erotic things I've ever seen."

He stared at me. Defiantly, I wiped tears away and refused to look in his direction. What did he expect me to say?

"However, I have a confession." Now, the humor left his voice and I noticed how pale his skin was for some reason. "You let your guard down while he kissed you, and I went into your mind and I saw everything. What your life has been like, I couldn't even begin to imagine, but I swear now on my kingdom and my life, you'll never be hurt again. I'm going to talk to Roman, and give you a few minutes to calm down," Caine said quietly, handing me a handkerchief and shutting the door of the truck.

I should be mad that he had invaded my privacy like that. But in all honesty, I was just glad someone knew. That maybe now I would finally be safe.

Doors opening a few minutes later alerted me that the guys were back. I wiped the tears off my face and tried to act nonchalant.

Roman sighed and sat in the seat behind me. "I'm sorry, I tricked you. The pouch I gave you was actually a truth potion. I needed to know if we could actually trust you. I honestly didn't expect those words to come out of your mouth. I do realize that you are not here to hurt us and that you just wanted a new life. It won't happen again."

Roman did sound sorry, and I probably should have been more upset he had tricked me like that. I was more upset that he had interrupted my first kiss. It probably meant nothing to Deagan, but it had meant the world to me. There was no way in hell though that I would bring that up. I was still pissed over it.

"It's fine. Can we just go now?" I snapped back.

I know I should have been a little nicer, but I was beyond the point of caring. I just wanted to get as far away as I could from the King, then get the hell away from them before I became anymore attached than I already was.

I leaned my head back and pretended to be trying to sleep. A few times they cleared their throats, but I ignored them. Too much had happened too fast, I needed time to process my feelings.

CHAPTER SEVEN

Rory

*J*erking awake, I rubbed my eyes as I felt the truck starting to slow. Looking around, I saw that we were stopping beside a small cabin.

"What are we doing?" I asked my voice still crackly from sleep, causing me to cough in an attempt to clear it.

"The Gargoyle castle is about ten minutes down the road. We can't take the truck any farther or we'd risk getting caught. Who knows what we're going to run into once we get in there," Deagan said as he pulled beside the cabin.

Looking at the clock, I saw that it was now fifteen after six in the afternoon. Wow, I had slept through the whole trip. The sun was still up but was starting its descent, which may not be a good thing.

"Do you think it's a good idea to go in at night since Roman is in pain then?" I spoke as the thought popped into my head. I could tell by the looks on their faces that they hadn't even thought about that.

See, I could be useful. Wait, where did that thought come from? I didn't want to be useful, I wanted to just get away. Didn't I?

"That's actually a really good point," Caine's voice had a hint of surprise to it as if he was shocked that I had actually had a good idea. *What a douche nugget!* "We either need to get there as soon as possible or camp out here until morning. Maddox won't care if we stay in his cabin. I vote we go in as soon as possible."

"I'll go with whatever you all decide," I said.

I hoped we could save him. From what I had overheard of Maddox, from my room, he seemed like a fun and nice person.

Roman seemed lost in thought for a long minute. "The only way we'll find him is through magic. Using my link to him would be the best way to do it."

"You're the mage. Should we go at night or during the day?" Caine asked, frowning.

After a minute, Roman said, "We should go at night. I'll be able to track Maddox easier when the pull and pain are at its strongest. I'll need to come up with a spell to make myself silent. If we go in, they'll hear me instantly. The pain's hard to explain but it's not something I can keep quiet about."

"Then, it's a plan," Caine said.

We unloaded out of the truck and Roman turned and headed inside the cabin.

"We'll go in, get washed up, and eat, but then we'll have to get moving. The sun will be down soon and Roman won't be any help when it does. Deagan, show Rory where she can freshen up, and I'll whip you all up something to eat." Caine grabbed his bag and headed towards the cabin leaving me alone with Deagan.

Embarrassment filled me, I didn't know how to act. Did I mention the kiss? Act like nothing happened? Or kiss him again? I knew which one I wanted to do, but even my hormone filled brain realized how stupid that idea was. A cough brought my attention to the gorgeous troll beside me.

"I can show you where to go, but do you want to talk first?" Deagan said, his eyes pleading with me to listen to whatever it is he wanted to say.

"Yeah, sure. What's up?" I shrugged attempting to act like I wasn't waiting with bated breath to see what he was going to say.

"I just wanted to let you know I don't usually attack girls on the side of the road. I'm still not sure why exactly I acted that way. There is just something about you," he replied, scooting closer until he was so close that all I could see was him.

My breath caught in my throat as his earthy scent made its way to me. I leaned in closer as he continued leaving me even more breathless.

"And I want more." He closed the gap between us and pressed his lips to mine.

I moved my hands up to his hair and pulled him as close as I could to me.

"Are you coming or not?" Caine yelled out completely killing the vibe. I really hated that damn vampire. Talk about a cock block. *Wait, was it a cock block when he blocked the girl?* Maybe I should ask him.

"We should go in. I wouldn't put it past him to come to get us." Taking my hand in his, Deagan headed towards the cabin.

I don't know how he could act all nonchalant, I was completely freaking out. *Were my hands clammy? Could he hear how fast my heart was beating?*

Snapping myself back to reality, I focused on Caine. It was about time that I gave him a piece of my mind.

"The bathroom is just through that door. Shout at me if you need anything. I'm going to find Roman." Deagan leaned down and gave me a quick kiss on my cheek before turning and walking away. It was such a cliche but damn, it was nice to watch him leave. His ass was perfection.

"I don't know how you did it, but you actually turned our scary, psychotic troll into a lovesick puppy. It's kind of off-putting, but also makes me curious. Are you a witch? Did your kiss put him under some kind of spell? I guess I'll just need to find out for myself." Caines sudden appearance should have surprised me, but I had a feeling this vamp was always lurking in the shadows.

Before I could reply to his insane accusations, he pulled me towards him and pressed his lips to mine. Opening my mouth to bite his lip, he took it as an invitation to invade my mouth with his tongue. Heat engulfed me, but I was also furious. I tried to shove him off, but he shrugged it off and deepened the kiss.

My knees went weak, and I could feel his hand on my back, pressing me close to him, his hard length throbbing against my stomach. I moaned as I felt my back slam into the wall, and he pulled my legs around his waist. The pure pleasure that shot through me as he rubbed his throbbing hardness against my center.

Breaking the kiss, I moaned and his red eyes pierced me. I was frozen as I stared at his perfect face, his fangs elongated and for some reason, I wanted to run my tongue over them.

"You ready to go, guys?" Roman yelled from another room, once again effectively killing the mood. One of these days I wasn't going to get fucking interrupted.

CHAPTER EIGHT

Maddox

"*I* will fucking end you! You sadistic son of a bitch! Torture me all you want, you will never take my kingdom," I screamed out at Richard. This dude was certifiable. He really thought he would be able to kill all of us off and no one would realize?

Richard had done far worse than just lock me in my stone form. The ring had been cursed to make me rock in the day, then at night I was back in human form, but I was paralyzed. Richard had taken complete advantage of that and had me tortured in unspeakable ways throughout the nights.

"Aww, Maddox. It's so cute that you think so but I have already won. Don't you see you're already dead? This little party is just for fun. Locking you in your Gargoyle form was genius, but having you completely powerless while I have my fun makes all those years pretending to care for you almost worth it," Richard laughed out as I cringed. How could we not have known that he was a crazy bastard hellbent on taking over everything?

"Fuck you!" I yelled out as he ran a serrated knife down my arm. Gritting my teeth, I just barely kept myself from screaming at the pain of my skin being ripped open. Just as quickly as it started the pain stopped as the wound started to heal.

Confusion set in at the fact that he was allowing me to heal, every other night he tortured me until I turned to stone at first light. Looking over at him, the look on his face made me realize that whatever was going to happen next was going to be worse than anything else he had put me through.

"Someone's going to figure out what you've done."

"By someone you mean THREE GUYS? Sorry, but they're safely at their homes. No one is coming for you."

I don't say it, but I have this crazy feeling they know. We've always had this connection. Something unexplainable between us.

"It's actually a fascinating story, one I so rarely get to tell." He grinned as my eyes caught movement by the doorway. I couldn't stop the instant relief as I saw Deagan, Roman, and Caine. "Once upon a time, there was an evil sorcerer who was infuriated when he wasn't invited to celebrate the coming of age of the first Princess Rory and future Queen of the Kingdom of the Fae." While he was speaking, I watched as all the guys got a shocked look on their face and looked behind them. "He took his revenge by cursing everyone who had attended. The Four Kings lost their Queens, the Princes lost their memories of each other and the beautiful princess who they had fallen for that very day. The King and Queen of the Fae, who had just announced that their daughter would become the next Queen, were slain where they stood and finally, the beautiful new Princess was taken and hidden away. All memory of her was erased and she got to live out her life as a servant that was cursed to be invisible inside of a castle. Visible to only those who caused her harm." There was a quiet feminine gasp at his words, but I had to be hearing things.

Again, subtly, I pulled at my restraints. Were they growing loose? "Interesting tale, old man."

Anger flashed in his eyes. "Oh, but it isn't a tale. It's the story of your pathetic life."

"I don't believe you."

His gaze bore into mine. "I'm no longer hiding the truth from you, so why bother hiding it from yourself?"

I knew he wanted a reaction, but I had none. At one point or another since we had become friends each of us had complained about the feeling of something missing. Realizing it wasn't something, but someone was horrible. He had taken our mothers, ruined our fathers as we had once known them and god only knows what had happened to the Princess. What a life she must have had.

I would destroy this man, I didn't know how or when but I knew his death would be at my hands. The sound of an engine filled the air, someone was coming. This was my chance to escape, as long as it wasn't the King's butt boy, Jeffrey.

"Oh, don't get too excited there, boy. That's just Jeffrey. You see my plans for you are coming to an end. Once I rid the world of the Gargoyle Prince, I can focus on eliminating those disgusting vampires. I will rule all and there is nothing you can do about it. My only regret will be not killing Caine, Deagan and little Rory while you watch. Maybe I should have killed Rory first since she's the only one who can end the curse I put on you. I truly am a genius. The only way you can be saved from being stone forever is a kiss from the girl who can't remember a thing about you," He laughed maniacally as he stepped away from the table that I was tied down on.

Frantically, I searched for a way to escape.

Looking toward the doorway, I felt a moment of relief as my eyes met Roman's. Before I could react, he rushed into the room, a huge sword in his hands. There was no noise other than the swish of the blade as he impaled his father through the stomach and jerked it back out.

Richard stared in shock as he fell to the ground. "Why?"

"Because I know what you truly are now." A look of pain came and went across Roman's face.

Blood leaked from Richard's mouth as he sputtered out the words, "I wish I'd killed you."

"And I wish I would've killed you a long time ago!" Roman raised the sword and brought it down as if he was going to behead his father, but then Richard vanished. and the sword embedded into the wooden floor.

"No!" I shouted.

I couldn't fucking believe it, we almost had him.

"Are you okay?" Deagen asked as I felt my entire chest clench.

"No, I'm not okay. Just untie me please," I said looking anywhere in the room, but at him.

My breath froze when my eyes landed on a girl that had her arms around Roman. I could hear her whispering something to him, and it stopped me in my tracks. There was just something about her, her face pulled and sad with blonde hair that had fallen from the bun.

CHAPTER NINE

Rory

I was still reeling from the confession that had come out of the King's mouth, but I just couldn't deal with that at the moment. Roman needed me. His face was crestfallen as he continued to stare at the spot where his father had just been. We had told him how his father was, but hearing it and seeing it were two different things.

Walking over to him, I pulled him down to me and engulfed him with my arms. I wouldn't admit it, but I needed the hug just as much as he did. My mind was racing from one thing to another, but in his arms, it finally slowed down until the only thing I was thinking about was that I hoped my hug comforted him as much as it did me.

"Are you going to be okay?" I whispered to him as I blocked out everything else that was going on in the room.

"No, I'm not okay. You all told me how he was, but as bad as it is to say I could hardly believe it. Hearing him talk about all that he had done though, broke something in me and now all I can think about is how can I make him pay, and get our memories back." With each word, his voice wavered more and more.

What made sense though was why I felt so strongly about these men. I guess some part of me had remembered what my brain couldn't. This whole thing just sent me reeling and I couldn't process it right now.

"So, yeah I still can't move. I figured the reason they tied me down was because of the fact that I would struggle, but here I am still laying on this fucking table when all I want to do is get the hell out of here," Maddox sounded angrier with each word, making me release Roman and get my first good look at him. His purple hair and dark eyes took me by surprise. I had never seen a person other than humans do their hair in those colors.

My eyes widen as I take in the mage king's words, what is so powerful about my kiss? Did I want to kiss Maddox? *Hell yes, I did.*

Touching my lips with my fingertips, I wonder if it will be the same as it was with Deagan and Caine.

"Um, yeah. I think I have to kiss you to fix that issue. I've already kissed two guys today, what's one more?" I said once again going for nonchalant and failing. You could hear the quiver in my voice as I stepped closer to the table he was laid on.

"You must be Rory then," was all that Maddox said as he looked at me expectantly, waiting for me to fix the issue.

When I was right beside the table, his breathing sped up. I could see it in the way that his muscular chest was rising and falling. Taking my hand, I laid it on his hard chest and leaned down to press my mouth against his. This was the first time I had ever initiated a kiss, but it didn't take long before Maddox responded. His lips parted and I hesitantly met his tongue with mine. I wasn't sure how into this kiss I needed to be for the spell to break, but I had no problem giving it my all as the all too familiar heat took over my body.

I ran my hand over his muscles, feeling his silky smooth

skin as I caressed his chest and abs. I knew the instant the curse broke. He growled and then his hands found my neck and the other found my ass as he pulled me on top of him. Completely oblivious to the fact that the other three guys were just standing there watching.

Roman cleared his throat. "I think the spell's broken... we should probably head back to the cabin before Richard comes back with reinforcements."

Fucking hormones were going to get me killed.

Breaking the kiss, I climbed off of him and felt my cheeks turn bright red. I matched the others in the room though as they all looked away embarrassed.

"Alright, Let's blow this joint. We have to get back to my castle and warn my dad. There's no telling what Richard will do now," Caine said before making his way out of the door.

I was more than a little unsure of what I needed to do now. I didn't want to leave them. But did they want me to stay with them? Yeah, the crazy bastard had said we were all connected in some way, but that didn't really change anything. Did it?

Luckily for me, the decision of leaving was taken from me as Roman walked over to me and put his hand in mine.

"You coming?" he asked as if he was unsure of what I was going to do.

I thought about how it felt to be around them, and the heat that had been in every kiss. Even with everything that had happened, I knew I didn't want to leave them. From the second I had climbed into that truck, I had wanted to be with Deagan and Roman. Caine was a giant asshole, but there was something about him that drew me to him, the same thing with Maddox, all we had done was kiss, but I wanted more.

"Of course," I answered squeezing his hand and pulling him out the door.

The ride back to the vampire castle had been mostly uneventful. Maddox explained everything that had happened since he was imprisoned. I was more than 99% sure that he left out a lot of the torture by telling us that he couldn't remember most of it. However, as he talked about it his eyes told me he was lying. He had suffered horrendously at the King's hands, but he was safe now and somehow I knew we would help him heal.

The castle was huge, I had been hidden when they had picked up Caine earlier. So this was the first time I had seen it up close.

We had just gotten out of the truck when loud angry voices reached us. Apparently, King Jacques was furious and yelling at someone that they hadn't looked hard enough for Caine. It should be loads of fun to tell him what happened while he was gone…not.

Everyone was standing around the fountain in the courtyard as we approached. A few of the servants turned as we arrived, but the king was lost to his yelling. It was clear to see that he loved his son and set my mind at ease about being here.

"Dad. Stop yelling, I'm right here. We need to talk, now, about King Richard. The blood oath has been broken and I hope from the bottom of my heart, you didn't know what he was up to." Caine looked a little worried as he spoke.

The King, however, looked completely confused. I was really praying that Caine's dad really was clueless about the extent of Richard's evil.

It was as if he finally understood that his son was standing in front of him, and before he said anything he quickly walked over and pulled Caine into a tight hug. It was a beautiful moment, his reaction something I had never really seen before and I found myself feeling a touch weepy.

"You get your ass inside, we'll talk there. I already explained why you needed to take the oath. We don't know how many of our enemies are lurking in the shadows." He let go of Caine and walked away.

Turning towards the Castle, we all followed the King silently. Not knowing how he would react, or how much he had been privy to, was clearly weighing on Caine's mind. We were about to find out though.

CHAPTER TEN

We were in the throne room; it was set in rich tones of gold and red. The king was sitting on his throne with his head in his hands. He had just found out what we had learned today.

"I knew he wasn't a good man, but I didn't know the extent of what was going on. I will need some time to fully process this. There are some books in the library that may be able to help you regain your memories, but I just need some time," King Jacques said pulling me out of my thoughts.

"I'm sorry, father," Caine said.

"None of it's forgivable," the king said, staring into his empty glass. "But my queen...knowing what happened to her breaks my heart all over again. I need... some time to think."

"Of course," Caine said.

We all rose as the King set down his drink and left the room.

It was heartbreaking. He had read Caine's mind and learned of the events that had happened today. It was safe to say that he was utterly broken.

My heart broke for him, but the relief I felt over the fact that he wasn't part of Richard's plans was tremendous.

"I'll go grab some of the books that he was talking about. You guys know the way to my rooms. I'll meet you there," Caine stated before also leaving the room.

Both Deagan and Roman grabbed my hands and led me to Caine's bedroom, Maddox following behind. I was wholly unprepared for what I saw when I got there. The room was painted in a light baby blue with a mural of the sun setting over a beach covering the largest wall. His furniture was light brown and looked like it had all been hand made. The dark red sheets on his king size bed were the only thing in there that looked remotely like I had expected.

"This is gorgeous," My voice took on a hint of wonder as I walked over to the beautifully painted wall. Never in my life had I seen anything so amazing, but I couldn't be distracted.

"How are you feeling?" Maddox asked as he sat down on the bed.

"Well, I found out I was a Princess and that my parents were killed and I have no memories of any of it. I think it's safe to say I am not doing all that great," I replied stopping myself from the long rant that I had been about to go on.

"We are right there with you. I just don't understand why my father would do it." Roman was staring at me intensely with his black eyes as if trying to memorize my face.

"Maybe it had something to do with the fact that there are four of you and one of me. I mean, how does that even work?" Even though those were the thoughts running through my head, I hoped that they were okay with it.

"We will just have to be honest with one another, no secrets and just take it one day at a time." Deagan sat down beside Maddox as a hopeful look crossed his face.

"It may be weird, but I want it. With all of you."

God, that was embarrassing. I can't believe I admitted all

that. Weirdly, the last one I expected to answer did. Maddox looked nervous continuously rubbing his hands together before he stood up and looked at Deagan.

"I think it's safe to say that we all want you too, Rory." He offered me a smile before clearing his throat and looking at Deagan."

"Richard told me about the history of the trolls. And, uh, you're actually a King, stolen by the Mage King as a Child."

Wow. Poor Deagan. Everyone turned to look at him, worried about how he would react but he still looked emotionless.

"I know," was all he said before turning and walking towards the window. "Ever since I could remember King Richard would beat me, humiliate or starve me. It happened so many times that I guess my body became immune to it. That was when he would tell me all he had done to my family. Then he would laugh and say how the future King was his son's slave. He told me how worthless I was and how having me was the best trophy he could get. He knew he could do anything he wanted and I would stay. He had complete control over one of the only people in the world who mattered to me. As long as Roman stayed, I would stay. I may not have been the Prince I was meant to be, but I was a friend. I was in charge of Roman's safety and I would've died before betraying that." My heart broke with every word that he spoke, and it clicked with me because he knew my pain.

"What the fuck, Deagan?" Caine said from the door, startling us all. His red eyes showed how angry he really was.

"I don't want to talk about it, okay? Let's just figure out how to get our memories back and go from there." Deagan started making his way to Caine, taking the books out of his hands.

"Deagan?"

"No," his answer was absolute. "I won't discuss it further."

Roman looked as if he wanted to press the issue, but kept quiet. There was moisture in his black eyes as he stared at his best friend.

He handed us each one and they were all quickly engrossed in the one they had taken.

I, on the other hand, was extremely apprehensive. Terrified about what I would find out. I couldn't stop the thoughts that passed through my head. Even though my life had been hell, it was mine and I already knew what had happened. What if we get our memories back and what happened when I was younger was worse?

Fuck! I screamed in my head. This was not the time to be a pansy. Looking down at the book in my hand, I took a deep breath and started to read.

CHAPTER ELEVEN

"I found it!" Maddox yelled out scaring the shit out of all of us. We had all been reading for what felt like hours, and I was so glad it was over. My brain was starting to hurt from information overload.

"Well, what do we have to do?" I asked ready to get whatever it was over with. It was time to figure out what had happened all those years ago. Maybe I would even figure out what other kinds of powers I had.

"It's something that you almost did all on your own. You have to kiss us all. True love's kiss will break the spell," Maddox said as he shot a dazzling smile at me that made me catch my breath.

"So I need to kiss Roman? Is that going to work?" I asked shocked at the fact that it was something so simple. I don't know why I was so nervous because I had already kissed three of the guys. Roman made me nervous though, and I couldn't understand why.

Looking over at him, he almost looked worried. I had to kiss another hot guy. What was my life coming to? Oh well, time to put on my big girl panties and step up. We all needed our memories back if we were going to go after Richard.

Marching over to Roman I took his face in my hands and pulled him towards me. My mouth landing on his maybe a little too forcefully, but I didn't want to give him a second to change his mind.

The minute our lips touched, images flashed across my mind. My memories came back in full force, it was like watching a movie. I saw my parents and could feel the love coming from them. The ball that they held was gorgeous, I remember the first time I saw the guys. We spent the whole night dancing and talking. That was when I knew they were going to be it for me. My mother had told me that the fae usually had multiple mates, her's had all been killed over the years except for my father. The hardest thing to remember was Richard coming into our castle after the ball and not being able to move. My mother and father stood immobile as he took their heads. He had walked over to me and told me that he had plans for me, but not to worry I wouldn't remember any of this. Then it was as if that life ended and the new life had begun.

Pulling away from Roman, I could feel the tears making their way down my face. The horror of all the things that Richard had taken from me was too much. I tried to turn away from all the guys, but they stopped me. All four came around and engulfed me in a hug; I could see that their eyes were also full of unshed tears.

No one said a word as Maddox lowered his head to mine and kissed me. It wasn't a hard kiss, but a sweet one. It was slow, but I still felt the heat starting to rise. It made me realize that I didn't want to take it slow. I wanted them all as often and as much as I could have them because they had already been taken from me once.

I ran my tongue over his lips and he opened, letting me

in. That ended the sweetness, because it was as if we were all desperate to touch each other. I could feel multiple hands running over my body causing my core to start to throb.

Breaking the kiss, I pulled away panting and trying to catch my breath. I took a second to calm my racing thoughts, which was hard to do with them all still running their hands over my body.

"I don't want to wait any longer for you all to be mine. You've been taken from me once and I want you all to make me yours. Now!" I said moaning my last words as Caine pulled me against him.

"Are you sure?" Deagan asked hesitantly.

"I'm sure." I ran my hands up his arms and gripped the back of his neck pulling his lips to mine.

Pulling back from the kiss, I lifted my shirt over my head and the bra and gauze wrap followed right after. It was a heady feeling to play the part of seductress. Their eyes all flared with lust as I shimmied out of my pants and underwear. Standing there fully nude, I gave them a minute to look their fill before turning and making my way to the bed. I sat down on the edge and gave them a pointed look and that was all it took. Before I had time to process what was happening, all four of my gorgeous men were nude and holy fuck, were they perfect.

Caine was the first to make it over to me and he kneeled down in front of me and started leaving kisses on my thighs. Roman set behind me and nipped at my neck as Deagan and Maddox sat on either side and started caressing my breasts. My body was on fire, the feelings that were flowing through me were unlike any I had ever experienced before.

I almost screamed when Caine's mouth finally made its way to my throbbing center. My brain left the building as Deagan and Maddox took my nipples into their mouths, it was as if I was a throbbing body of need and the only thing I could think of was the pressure that was building in my core. Caine's finger pressed against my opening, teasing me.

My heart was racing. I tilted my head back and moaned just as Roman ravaged me with a kiss that made my head spin. He bit my lip just as Caine plunged a finger inside me. I gasped as he slid his finger in and out in a torturous rhythm.

My hands reached out and ran over Deagan and Maddox's stomachs until I was low enough to grab their engorged erections. They both groaned causing my nipple to vibrate just as Caine slid another finger inside of me. Moaning softly, it was a wonder I was able to think with his tongue and fingers working magic over me.

I gripped the cocks in my hands and started pumping faster as Caine curved his fingers slightly, hitting a spot that I never knew existed.

"Yes!" I screamed breaking my kiss with Roman as I shattered around Caine's fingers.

My release washed over me as he pulled his fingers out and slid them into his mouth. I gulped, watching him. I had never seen something so sexy and I knew for sure that I wasn't done with them, but before we could go farther a loud bang snapped us out of our lust filled thoughts.

All my men jumping to attention, ran out of the room before I could even blink. What the hell was that? Grabbing a discarded shirt, I ran after them terrified of what I would find. Had Richard come for us? Was he coming to take me back?

Smoke filled the lower level of the castle. A huge gaping hole, where the wall used to be. Confusion hit me as I noticed that nothing else seemed out of place. There was no one here, no Richard or any other threat. Just as I reached my guys, who looked just as confused as I felt, a loud piercing scream filled the room and they took off again towards the sound.

"Princess Ella is gone! She's gone! I went to check on her when I heard the explosion and all that was there was only this note." A servant handed the letter to Roman, his face twisted in shock and fear.

Caine took off towards what I could only assume was his sister's room, while Roman read the letter. It was at that moment, I realized they were all still butt ass naked. If this hadn't been so serious, I would have thought it was hilarious.

"Fuck. My dad has taken her. He says he won't let her go until Jacques sends us back to him. He shouldn't have been healed by now. It should have at least taken a whole day," Roman said looking gutted at the evil that his father had once again committed.

God, I can't believe this is happening now. For a small second, I'd thought I'd finally been given my happily ever after. But I should've known it was impossible. I would never be free until Richard was dead and everyone I loved was safe.

So I make a vow to myself, I will find him and I will kill him. Then, I will take my place as Queen and have the happy life I have always dreamed of.

A kiss woke me from my false life, and now I won't rest until I take what's mine.

Will Richard get his comeuppance? Will we find out just what has happened to Ella?

Find out the answers to these questions and more in our next Fairytale Retelling,

More Than A Slipper.

ABOUT THE AUTHOR

Beth Hendrix

Beth is a single mother of two, who has worked in a custom cabinet shop since she was young. She always has so many ideas flowing in her head but never thought that writing was a reality until some other amazing authors pointed out that she could. She loves all things paranormal, and has a very unhealthy obsession with chocolate and doughnuts. She can usually be found chasing after her kids, typing like a mad woman or lost in a book.

If you would like to stalk...I mean follow Beth and her crazy antics, she can be found here.

https://www.facebook.com/BethHendrixAuthor/ Facebook Page

https://www.facebook.com/groups/BethsDemonicReaders/ Facebook Group

Authorbethhendrix@gmail.com Email

Www.bethhendrixbooks.com Website

ABOUT THE AUTHOR

Alexis Taylor

Alexis is a mother of three, who can usually be found bossing around Nikki. She got lucky and her best friend forced her to write with her, and it is now something that she loves to do. She loves all things horror, and is a huge mystery buff. She can be found trolling Instagram for hot guys for inspiration, arguing with her young demons, obsessing over Averi Hope & Victoria Schafer's covers or falling into random things because she is ridiculously clumsy.

If you want to keep up with Nikki and Alexis, Join our Alexis and Nikki's Hellions group on facebook. You can chat directly with them, and get first looks at their new books/series.
Alexis and Nikki's Hellions

THE HUNT

By Jenée Robinson

Heat Level- A Little Bit Spicy

CHAPTER ONE

*T*he breeze ruffles the curtains of my canopy bed, and I stare at my love as he tosses and turns; bad dreams have overtaken him again.

Each night is the same: he slips into my bed wrapping his arms around me and warming me, until he starts to dream.

Rolling over to face him, I run my fingers through his white-blond hair. My hand trails down his cheekbone to his chin, enjoying the smoothness of his freshly shaved skin his lips draw my focus, pinched together in a scowl. He stills at my touch, but his eyes still flutter under their lids.

The only light in the room is the flickering flame of a candle on the table next to our bed. Even in the dim light I can see his eyes as they slowly blink open. Turning slightly, his gaze catches mine.

"I'm sorry, my love. Did I wake you again?" he whispers.

Of my three men, Evander is the most damaged. The beatings he endured as a child from not only his father, but his mother, left more than physical scars. Every night I lie awake, watching over him as he sleeps restlessly. Lying next to him, I'm helpless to stop them.

"I just wish I could take these nightmares from you," I say, my voice cracking a little.

"My mind has the scary capability of being dark and demented," he replies with a humorless laugh.

My heart aches for him, and the desire to take his pain away fills me as I caress his cheek. "Are you afraid of your dreams?" I ask softly,

He looks deeply into my eyes and his answer is little more than a whisper off his lips. "Yes."

"Don't worry, my love." I pull him closer to me, my tone earnest. "I'll protect you."

A smile tugs at his lips. "Then I shall only ever sleep in your arms."

Evander pulls me flush against him and lays his head on my chest. He closes his eyes, but the smile remains. Once his grip loosens I know he has drifted back to sleep. As I try to join him in slumber, my mind won't shut off. I think of Thane and Kristof and how the three of them are not only my lovers, but my best friends; we are each other's best friends. I never had the intention of falling in love with three men, but they accepted it willingly and reciprocated.

My mind wanders to being Queen. It has its perks — like bossing everyone around, but also has its downfalls — making decisions that effect my people. I make a mental note of what I need to accomplish in the following days.

I barely close my eyes and start to drift off when my door slams open, causing Evander to jump up and stand in front of me in a defensive stance, ever the gentleman. Uncaring of his nakedness.

"She is nearing the walls with a vast army. Come quickly! We must ensure your safety," my captain informs us.

"Give us a moment, the queen and I need to dress." Evander sits back down on the bed with me. "I'll escort her to the cabin myself and join you on the front line as soon as I can. Please collect Thane and Kristof."

"As you wish, Commander," the captain replies, then exits the room.

I crawl out of the bed and straddle him, looking him dead in the eye. "Evander, you can't face her without me. I can fight. I'm not some helpless woman."

He wraps his arms around my hips. "Don't fear. We'll defeat her, and the three of us will be back to you in no time."

Tears prick at my eyes, and I steady my voice before I reply. "You'd better, I'll never forgive you if you don't."

We dress in silence. Instead of the fancy, glamorous dress I normally wear, I don simple brown pants and a forest green tunic that almost mirrors Evander's.

He quickly adds his armor, and once he's finished, starts making his way over to me. He steps close and straps a sword belt around my hips, running his hand along the small of my back and laughing as I shiver slightly under his touch. Evander loves it when I can't hide my reaction to him.

"My queen, I love you with all my heart. Nothing and no one will keep me apart from you," he says, then kisses me until my head swims.

When he pulls back, I cling to his shirt and look up into his smiling face. *How did I get so lucky?*

I take his hand as we exit the room. "I guess we'll be heading to that cottage in the woods... unless you've decided to let me fight at your side?" I look at him with an eyebrow raised.

His laugh is like music to my ears. "Are you trying to sweet talk me? Because you must know, while I want you at my side, I *need* you to be safe."

We reach the castle doors and two black mares are waiting for us saddled and ready. Thane and Kristof have ahold of their bridles. Thane has been on perimeter duty, managing the soldiers and ensuring they stay awake at this hour. Kristof had been tasked to clear the villagers from the approaching army's path.

A smile forms on my lips; even in the dim light of the torch I can see the twinkle in Kristof's green eyes and the scowl Thane wears almost permanently. I'm glad I'll get to be with my three men one more time before I'm hidden away.

Evil is coming for me. She destroyed my father and vowed to do the same to me. Now is the time to be smart and not let my emotions control me.

My hand is still entwined with Evander's. I pull it from his, running my fingers down his palm as I do. It's only a few short steps before I reach Thane, and his arms open wide welcoming me against him in the safety of his embrace. I breathe in his woodsy scent, and my muscles instantly relax.

Thane pulls back just a little, holding my gaze. His brown eyes bore into mine and I see his chestnut locks wave a little in the breeze. "Be safe, my Queen. I'll count the moments until your return." He places a sweet kiss on the tip of my nose and my heart melts a little more...

A gagging noise comes from Kristof, and I turn to see a smile on his face. He stands almost a foot taller than I, and is the scruffiest of the three. His deep chocolate brown hair is slicked to the left with not a hair out of place. His facial hair is little more than a five o'clock shadow.

"You're just jealous that Thane doesn't talk to you the same way," I retort.

Kristof closes the distance between us handing the reins off to Evander just as Thane steps back. "That may be so, but I only have eyes for you."

Kristof wraps his arms around my waist and lightly presses his lips to my neck. Chills run down my spine, just from that one kiss.

"I wish there was a way all four of us could go together. I don't want to be without any of you." Worry twists my insides as I eye them.

A horn sounds in the distance, but it's still too close for comfort... She's almost here. My pulse speeds up. We need to go. *Now.* My kingdom is what she wants, but not to rule — to burn it to the ground.

Kristof lets go and helps me mount my horse. He places one last kiss on my hand before he swats my horse spurring her into a run toward the cottage. I turn for one last look at Thane and Kristof as I ride away from them. They both have a sad look on their face, and seeing this causes a tear to spill over and roll down my cheek.

I wipe it away before turning my attention back to Evander and my horse. I have to remind myself that this is for the good of my kingdom. If she were to get her hands on me, she would torture all my subjects before killing them, saving me for last to make me watch it all.

We ride hard and fast, knowing the path like the back of our hands, until the time we enter the forest. I slow my mare and we make a hard right, her pace little more than a trot. Evander and I don't speak, but we pull out our torches and light them almost simultaneously.

The trees crowd us where I am leading, and Evander follows. Torch in one hand and reins in the other, I also watch the path for branches that may have fallen. I can hear Evander's horse getting restless from the slow pace, but the last thing we need is to make a mistake. Not now.

Finally, I see a glint of the window illuminated by the torch light and breathe a sigh of relief. We've made it safely.

Stiffening, I suddenly can't catch my breath. So this is where I'll be hidden safely away, while Evander, Thane, and Kristof will be battling to save my kingdom. It feels wrong. I know it's for the best... but I don't like it.

I dismount from my horse and tie the lead to a post on the side of the cottage, then extinguish my torch. When I turn around, Evander is right there. For one moment I see it in his eyes, his fear. His worry about leaving me here alone. But Evander is a warrior, his emotions are there and gone in an instant.

Reaching out, he touches my face. His fingertips on my flesh awaken everything within me, and my body remembers our night together. I remember every kiss, every touch, every powerful moment where time seemed to stand still.

He pulls me against him, his embrace rough and needy. When his lips crush mine, I feel his emotions flowing through me, saying the words he's unable to express.

He steps back, and I almost reach out and pull him back to me.

But I can't bear to draw this out. To make this harder for him.

He mounts his horse and pierces me with a fierce stare. "I love you," he says, his tone gruff.

I wrap my arms around myself in a hug as he rides away. Tears spill down my face when I enter the cottage, and I let them be.

Lighting a few candles on my way to the bed, I sit and try to clear my mind. Too many negative thoughts have made their way in. All my subjects and my men dead, my kingdom destroyed.

I blame my father; he was an idiot. He is the reason for all of this. You don't piss off a mage, and he did just that. She destroyed him, just as promised. She also told him she would do the same to me until our kingdom fell and we were forgotten.

My father was a fair and just ruler, but he feared magic and the mages who wielded it. He doomed us all with one action: outlawing magic. All mages were persecuted for just having magic... even if they didn't use it, no matter their status or age. That is, until the entire kingdom tried to kill the oldest and wisest mage, Lilthia.

Big mistake.

She first tried to curse me when I was just a brand-new babe. But the guards were ready for her, and her attack failed. Lilthia going after me drove my father mad, and he retaliated. But, of course, she was ready for him too. She turned herself into a dragon; they were no match for her.

But all that is in the past.

I lie back on the rickety bed and pull the thin blanket over me. It does nothing to ease the chill that has taken over my body. I close my eyes and try to clear my mind once more, but all I can think of is my men and my people, and I'm here hiding in this old cottage.

Grabbing a candle as I rise, I head to the front door and make my way outside to collect a few pieces of wood from the pile that we'd gathered a few days ago. I take them straight to the hearth and lay them down. Setting the candle on the table, I then go to work stoking the embers.

The light from the fire illuminates the cottage once lit, and I stand in front of the it trying to rid my body of the chill. Unhooking my sword belt from my waist, I stride over to the bed and lean my sword against the table, before I crawl beneath the sheets.

The bed creaks and groans as I struggle to get comfortable. I'm not used to sleeping alone, and my thoughts are filled with my men; are they still safe?

Did I make a mistake in coming here?

But as the hours tick by, my thoughts grow sluggish. Yes, I had woken only hours before, but before last night I hadn't slept in days. I hear a familiar, evil laugh as I am drifting off to sleep, and I jolt fully awake.

I grab my sword as I spring up and out of bed.

Shit, has she found me?

The wind carries the mage's voice to me. "Queen Rose, you cannot hide from me. I have taken your father; next, I will take your men. I hope you kissed Evander goodbye. He's mine now."

Racing from the cottage, sword in hand, I almost have the reins free from the post when I hear a stampede of horses approaching. No time to run, so I must fight. Even if it kills me.

But instead, I hear two familiar voices calling my name. Thane and Kristof.

"I'm here! I'm safe!" My nerves calm just a bit until I can make out Thane's next words.

I close the distance between his horse and myself.

"Rose, she took him. She took Evander," Thane says as he dismounts his horse. He wraps an arm around my waist, ushering me back into the cottage.

"No, we can't just… just go inside. We need… Evander. It's Evander! We need to get him back! I don't want to think about what torture she has planned for him."

"I agree, Rose. Evander told us no matter what happens we are to take care of you. Rest is essential. We can't fight Lilthia when we are exhausted. I promise we'll rise early, grab supplies, and start our search. We'll not be any good to him dead on our feet," Thane says, climbing into the small bed.

I turn and see Kristof nodding in agreement. "In this darkness it would be too hard to track them. First light we will be ready to start the hunt."

Frowning, I know he is right. "How did she get her nightmarish hands on him?"

"The three of us were on the front line, side-by-side fending off her legion," Kristof says. "Out of nowhere, I felt a blast of energy hit me; I flew back several feet from the position I was just in. I got up and ran back to where I had just been standing. As my steps reached the spot I was flug from, I saw her. Lilthia seemed to be floating on air and her attention was focused on Evander. She must have bewitched him; he stood there like an idiot. She glided right up to him, then with a snap of her fingers he fell over her shoulder and they were gone."

My mind is distraught over the news, and tears stream down my cheeks. Kristof wraps me in his warm embrace and vows, "We will retrieve him."

Thane doesn't say a word as he watches us. I look at him and he gently pats the spot on the bed next to him.

"I don't think rest will come so easy knowing he is out there with her." I eye Thane and place my hands on my hips.

I carefully crawl in next to him and Kristof follows. I snuggle up against Thane's chest with Kristof behind me, and sleep comes easier than I thought it would.

CHAPTER TWO

*a*s dawn breaks through the dirty window, I stretch and knock Kristof to the floor. My hand does little to stifle my laugh or hide my smile. Then the memories of last night come flooding back. I jump up with purpose.

"I love you too, my queen." He laughs as he climbs to his feet.

"Let us head to the castle for supplies. We need to start our search now," I say as I fasten my belt and gather my bag from the floor.

"My queen, are you coming with us?" Thane looks up at me, still lying on the bed.

"Of course. Lilthia messed with the wrong queen. If she wants me, she'll have to fight me. I'll not let her take one of you and not suffer the consequences. Now move your ass, we are wasting daylight," I reply.

Thane jumps up and readies the horses while Kristof douses the fire.

Kristof and I join Thane outside. He has my mare untied and ready for me to mount. As I climb up on her I thank him.

Once I settle in my saddle, they ascend their horses,

and we head back to my kingdom. The trek is much faster, down limbs are much easier to spot in the daylight. I slow a little as I approach the little town that lies right outside my castle walls. With my mission on my mind, I enter the gate with motivation. It is a welcome sight to see my captain is standing at the front doors awaiting me.

"Captain, please follow me. We have a lot to discuss and little time to do it," I say, still walking.

He follows. "Yes, my lady."

"I need three fresh horses. Thane, Kristof, and I are going to hunt down Lilthia. Coming for me — I get, but she's crossed the line by taking Evander."

He stops in his tracks. "My queen, do you think it is wise to leave the kingdom with no ruler?"

I turn to look at him. "Inform them I am ill. There is no reason they need to know I am not here."

I continue on to my chambers, and he trails behind still assaulting me with questions. "As you wish, my queen. What else do you need from me?"

"Please send Iris in. I am leaving my people in your hands. Care for them as I would; I would trust no other with all this power. Thank you, Captain, for your loyalty."

"As you wish, my queen. I will not let you down." He bows as he exits my chambers.

A few moments later I hear a light tapping on my door.

"Enter," I command.

My beautiful, fair-skinned, red-haired handmaiden enters. "You wanted to see me, my Queen?"

"Yes, thank you for coming so fast, Iris. I need more outfits like the one I am donning. Also, any dried meats or fruits that will not spoil. I am unsure how long we will be gone. Any supplies that you think will be helpful but not too heavy would be great."

"I will quickly gather it all," she says, exiting the room in a hurry.

Freshening up seems like a good idea before we embark on this adventure, so I make my way to my wash basin and use my rag to cleanse my body of last night's excursion through the forest.

I am pulling on fresh pants as my door opens, and I scramble to get them fully on.

I look up to see a smile on Kristof's face, and I feel like an idiot that I'm pulling up my pants so fast, yet my top is bare.

Placing my hand on my hips, I scold him. "Have you ever heard of knocking before you enter? It's common courtesy. You should try it."

"If I had knocked, I wouldn't have seen this glorious sight before me," he counters.

I narrow my eyes at him. "Always the smooth talker, aren't you?"

As he takes a few steps toward me, the light coming in from the window highlights the red in his hair. It still amazes me that it does that; I want to run my fingers through it. Then I remember I'm shirtless and stop myself.

I hear the rumble of laughter in his chest as I pull on my top. "We don't have time for games. We need to find Evander and stop Lilthia."

"You are right, my lady. I meant no disrespect. I have come to let you know that all the bedrolls and tents are packed, and the horses are ready."

I nod to him. "As soon as Iris arrives with the supplies I asked for, I will be ready."

He steps toward me, lightly skimming my cheek with the side of his hand. "I shall always wait for you."

He knows how to turn me to putty in his hands. I place my hand in his and smile sweetly at him. "Go make sure Thane is ready."

He gives me a sour look and retreats from my chambers.

After a few more minutes Iris is back with a bag.

"Thank you, Iris," I say as she hands it to me. "You are speedy, as always."

She bows a little. "My queen, please stay safe on your travels. I hope and pray for your quick return."

"Thank you, Iris. I have to get Evander back and stop Lilthia's reign of terror once and for all. We can no longer live in fear."

"I agree. This is no way to live."

She opens my chamber door for me, closing it behind us as we walk in silence to the front entrance. Thane and Kristof are holding the reins of three brown horses, and they both smile as they see me step out.

My guys and the captain bow as I reach them. "Everyone ready? Captain, please take care of my subjects. We will return as soon as possible."

"Take care, my queen, and be safe. They will never know of your absence," he assures me.

"Thank you," I reply as I mount my horse. I look over to Thane and Kristof. "Ready guys? We are burning daylight."

We start at a slow trot, heading north.

Kristof pulls up on my left, his light brown hair blowing in the wind. "Where to, my queen?"

I smile at him. "I think our best bet is to go to the local village two day's ride from here. Head to the tavern and listen for talk of Lilthia. See if we can get some leads on her location."

"That is a good plan. So ride till dusk, set up camp, and then do it all over?" he asks.

"Basically, yes. Now let us see how fast this horse can run," I call out as I spur my horse onward.

Thane is leading us, and I am grateful for that. I am familiar with this route but not as much as I'd like to be.

Ruling means I am secluded to my castle and the little village that surrounds it.

It's freeing to ride in the open. But I'm not too carefree, we still need to be cautious... One never knows all the secrets the trees may hold.

We have been riding a few hours when I spy a glint of gold not too far ahead. Just as I call out to Thane, an arrow whirls past his head. It sticks out of a tree just to my left.

"Thane, faster! Someone has you in their sights," I command.

Kristof strings his bow and begins to launch arrows in the direction of the shooter.

This gives me the distraction I need to push my horse to her limit, and she obeys. I have her gallop just past where the arrow came from, and then I jump off my horse and send her to gallop on, I then as quietly as I can and run for the spot where I saw the glint.

I release my sword from the belt on my side and sneak up on the archer. The point of my sword is now at the base of his neck, and I apply just a little pressure.

"Drop the bow and slowly turn around. Try anything, and I will gut you were you stand," I tell him.

He does the smart thing and drops the bow, keeping his hands open where I can see them. I pull the tip of my sword back just enough where he can turn to face me but not get sliced in the process.

I give him a once over. He's in need of a haircut; his shaggy brown hair almost covers his brown eyes — which are looking at the ground — and his face has a shadow where he hasn't shaved.

"Why were you firing arrows at us?" I demand.

His eyes snap up, and I can see the recognition in them. He knows who I am.

Before he can kneel, I move the tip of my sword from his neck to directly over his heart.

"Do not move. I asked you a question. Will you not answer me?"

"My queen, I didn't know who I was shooting at. I saw what I believed to be three men on horseback. I shot because it has been days since my last meal. I was hoping to hit the bags for any scraps that may be in them," he replies.

I lower my sword and look to Kristof. "Throw him a few coins and some of the dried meat. Let us be on our way."

"Thank you, my queen. I do not deserve your good will. I pledge my sword and bow to you, if you will have me," the man says.

"I don't trust him," Thane speaks up.

"Why would you, he shot at you?" I retort.

Kristof stifles a laugh. "He will have to prove his worth, but we don't need another mouth to feed."

"He can have half my food, and he will earn his place. He is one of my subjects, and I will not leave him to starve," I tell them.

I turn back to face the stranger. "What is your name? You are welcome to travel with us to the next town. If you cross me, make no mistake, I will gut you myself and not bat an eyelash."

He nods. "My name is Laken."

With that, I turn and start walking back to my horse. As I glance over my shoulder, I notice that Thane and Kristof are on either side of him, eyeing him with mistrust.

I laugh a little as I climb back on my horse. "Thane, since he likes you so much, I say he rides with you. Laken, don't forget your bow."

I hear a groan escape Thane's lips, but he doesn't argue. I have to suppress a laugh as I see Thane mount the horse and Laken join him. Laken sits awkwardly on only half the saddle as it was meant for one rider. With no real handholds in sight he has to hold onto Thane.

Kristof takes the lead and we are back on the mission to find Evander.

Our horses trot with ease on the worn roads, and even though I have pushed my horse to ride fast and hard, I don't want to overwork her. I do not know how far our journey will take us, and I will need a great steed to get me there.

Even in the cool breeze the sun's rays beat down on me, causing sweat to pool on my lower back.

The trees start to get thicker with each step of my horse, the lush greenery a wonderful change from the interior of castle walls. I even spy several different types of flowers growing around or near their base.

The rush of water catches my ear, and I call to Kristof, "I think here is a good place to water the horses and give them a rest."

He nods and exits the worn road, disappearing into the row of trees just ahead of me. I pull the reins and follow where he leads, just on the other side of the trees to the stream I heard mere minutes ago.

Thane and Laken are only a few steps behind, and as soon as their horse stops, Laken scrambles off as fast as he is able, almost falling in the process.

Thane walks up to me, pulling me in close and kissing me. Once he ends the kiss, I am pulled from his arms and into Kristof's. He repeats the same actions as Thane. He ends the kiss and takes my horse toward the water to drink.

"Marking your territory, are we boys?" I ask with an eyebrow raised.

Kristof just shrugs and Thane snorts and replies, "Maybe."

I roll my eyes and take a seat in the shade of an over-grown tree, enjoying a moment's peace from the heat of the sun. Pulling a few pieces of meat from my pack, I offer one to Laken. He hasn't taken his eyes off me since he dismounted Thane's horse.

He thanks me and takes a seat next to me. I cock my head to the side and address him. "Tell me the tale that is Laken."

CHAPTER THREE

*H*is dark brown eyes bore into me as he starts to speak, so much so I have to glance away.

"Not much to tell, your majesty. My parents were simple farmers for your kingdom. They have been done right by your father, and you when you came to rule. Once I was old enough, I signed up for the royal guard. I barely made it through training, something about my lack for respecting authority failed me. I served the crown for many years until me and one of my commanders didn't see eye to eye. My superiors decided it was best I take my leave."

He pauses for a few moments before continuing. "I have spent the time after that just traveling the kingdom, working for scraps. Too ashamed to return home and face my parents. My mother's disappointment would crush me."

I can feel the honesty in his words.

"What did you and your superiors disagree on?" I ask as I raise my eyes to meet his.

He shrugs. "I'm unsure if it is my place to tell, my queen."

"Of course, if you truly believe that I am your queen, you will tell me."

"My superiors took me along with a troop of men to a village a few day's ride from where we were stationed. Men were fighting over land, killing each other. When we arrived there was a full on battle going on, farmer against farmer. Once we broke up the fight and talked some sense into the farmers, the superiors decided to celebrate." He stops again.

He looks down, until I place a hand over his. His eyes bore into mine.

"Tell me what they did," I command, my tone neutral but authoritative.

"I tried to stop a couple of the men who flung women over their shoulders. They weren't laughing, tears stained their cheeks. I was told to mind my own business. I didn't listen and I was stripped of my sword and told not to return."

"When I return to the castle, I would very much like a word with these so-called superiors of yours. That is not acceptable for my men or my kingdom."

I rise, dusting off my pants, and make my way over to my horse and my men. They were eyeing Laken the whole time we were talking.

I pat Thane's shoulder. "Ready to continue? Are you still willing to share your horse with Laken? Or I could," I suggest, batting my eyelashes.

Thane and Kristof both puff out their chests some, and with that I have to stifle a laugh.

Kristof speaks up, "My queen, would you be willing to share your horse with me?"

"Aww, are you taking pity on poor Thane here?" I laugh. "Yes, of course I would love to share my horse with you."

I climb up and pat the spot behind me, motioning to Kristof to join me. I don't have to pat it more than once before he jumps on.

I turn my horse to face Laken. "Kristof was gracious enough to share my horse, so you can ride his. Let us head out; we still have a big journey ahead of us."

Laken carefully approaches Kristof's horse, raising his hand slowly to her nose. When she doesn't back up, he pats her side and then climbs on.

"It's about time, let's go," Thane huffs as he spurs his horse on and leads us north again.

The temperature has dropped a few degrees, and I shiver just a little prompting Kristof to wrap his arms tighter around me. His firm grip sets my exposed skin on fire. I lean back into him, and a little groan escape his lips.

I turn my head just enough to kiss his cheek; he returns with a trail of kisses down my neck. A cough comes from behind us, and my glance backward reveals a flush on Laken's cheeks.

"Oh how sweet, we've embarrassed Laken with our affection for each other," I say laughingly.

"Does that mean we should stop, my queen?" Kristof ponders, tapping his finger on his chin.

"Well, maybe just until we stop for the night," I reply.

The farther north we travel, the more the roads wind as the trees get thicker and closer to the road. It seems as if the roads were made to follow them, not the other way around.

I wish that I had thought to grab a coat, but Kristof's embrace will do just nicely.

Thane heads off the main road and into an unseen clearing, signaling we are stopping for the night. He hops down and ties his horse to a tree near a stream and some tall grass. Kristof follows suit and then extends a hand to me, helping me down from my horse. Still holding the reins, I tie them onto a tree next to Thane's horse and grab the pack that holds the tent and get to work.

Kristof and Thane do a perimeter check while Laken is off

gathering firewood. Once my guys return, they help me finish up the almost complete tent before setting up the fire pit.

I grab a rag along with clean clothes and head to the stream. I take a look around before I strip down to my under-things. Testing the water, I dip a toe in the stream. The current isn't too strong, so I plunge in one foot and gingerly place the other in before beginning to wash off the sweat and dirt from the day's adventure.

Humming to myself, I almost miss the snap of a twig to my left. I reach for my sword, grabbing only air. With only have a thin rag to cover me, I didn't think this through, I should have made one of my men come with me.

Tilting my head to the left to see Laken just standing there and staring. I swear I can see a little drool forming on his chin.

"Laken, it is not nice to stare," I politely remind him.

As if he is shaken from a trace, his gaze falls to the grass. "I'm am so sorry, my queen. I was headed back to camp and heard humming. Unsure of the origin, I thought I better check it out."

"Well if you've had a good view, head back to camp. I'm almost done here." I proceed to start washing again, but keep an eye on him as he retreats back to camp.

I slip into clean clothes similar to the ones I have been wearing. The colors are a little lighter on these, and I feel refreshed and ready for what's next.

As I approach camp, I get a whiff of meat cooking on the fire. My curiosity peaked, I step through the tree line, and find the three men sitting around the fire. Kristof is chatting with Laken and Thane sits opposite to them, his face wearing a scowl. When he sees me, a smile appears on his face.

"Miss me that much?" I ask as I take a seat next to him.

"More than you know," he says and pulls me in for a kiss.

We break apart and Kristof's eyes are on us while Laken's

are on the fire. I stand and make my way in between them. As Kristof moves closer, Laken scoots away; a smile tips my lips.

"What's so funny?" Kristof asks as he places a hand on the small of my back.

"I think Laken here is uncomfortable after getting an eye full at the stream." I snort out a laugh.

"What?" Thane and Kristof say in unison.

I look from Kristof to Thane. "Relax, I was washing up when Laken came upon me. It could've been anyone. He apologized and went on his way. No harm, no foul."

Kristof relaxes by my side, but I can still see the tension written all over Thane's body.

"Thane, let us take a walk. We have some things to discuss," I say.

He simply nods and follows me.

I take his hand in mine and we head back through the tree line, walking the edge of the stream.

"Thane, what is your distaste for Laken? He has not wronged you, yet you have hate for him written all over you."

He stops where he stands. "There is just something about him that rubs me the wrong way. I can't put a finger on why; it's just a feeling in my gut."

"We will part ways with him once we are in Ravenwallow. I haven't forgotten we are searching for Evander. Do not fear, we will be reunited again soon." I take his hand in mine and squeeze it gently, offering my reassurance.

"I know, my queen. This trip doesn't seem right without him," he replies.

"I agree."

We walk for a little while longer, enjoying each other's company. Even in this crazy life, we need to stop and appreciate what we have. As soon as I can feel that Thane has wound down, we head back to our makeshift camp.

Kristof has a smile on his lips and a cooked rabbit in his hands. He raises a leg toward me as I get closer. I take a bite as I grab it from his hand.

"Thank you, I'm starving," is all I manage as I stuff more into my mouth.

It doesn't take long for the food to disappear. We all clean up any mess that may be left. A bear in camp in the middle of the night wouldn't be a pleasant surprise.

"I'll take first watch," Laken offers.

"I will as well," Thane adds.

Laken just nods in acknowledgement. Thane doesn't trust him. I am a little grateful that camp will be protected by two men. Lilthia is still out there, and she is capable of anything. She has a sweet tongue and can bend men to her will easily. The only men I have seen able to resist her are my men: Evander, Thane, and Kristof.

Oh, Evander. I miss his cheeky smile and retorts, running my hands through that blond almost white hair. *I will get you back, my love.*

In the tent Kristof has laid out two bed rolls right next to each other, and he is naked in the middle.

I raise an eyebrow. "Don't you look inviting?"

"I just thought you'd want to snuggle with me." He looks up at me with a cheeky grin.

This causes my lips to tip up into a smile as well. "Snuggling is what you call it now? As much as I'd love to snuggle, I don't think it's the right time. Scoot over and I'll join you."

Before I lie down I remove my clothes and fold them, placing them neatly on my pack. With my sword in hand, I take my place on the bed rolls with Kristof. My sword gets placed on the grass just off to the side of the rolls. Being out in the middle of nowhere you never know when you'll have to defend yourself.

Kristof pulls me close, pushing his hard length between my thighs. A groan escapes my lips.

He kisses my neck and whispers in my ear, "I thought you just wanted to snuggle."

"I lay down innocently enough. You're the one trying to change my mind," I point out.

I close my eyes and lean into him, and he wraps his arms around me tighter, continuing the kisses, moving his hips just enough to tease me. He inches closer to my center. As another groan leaves my lips, I hear a cough.

My eyes snap open and none other than Laken is standing just inside the tent watching us.

I try to lighten the mood. "What, did you want to join us?"

His cheeks flush red and his glaze trails the floor. "I'm sorry, my queen, Thane and I heard movement to the north. You two may want to dress in case we have to move."

Kristof snorts. "You're a real buzz kill, but we shall dress and join you two in a moment."

I slip back into my shirt and pants, pulling my boots on as I grab my sword.

I reach for the flap of the tent as a hand reaches in. I take a step back and raise my sword.

Kristof mimics my stance; a worried look crosses his face.

"You can come out, or we will come in," a disembodied voice says.

Kristof nods and lowers his sword just a little and steps out before I do.

I make my way into the light to see a tied up Laken sitting on a log, his eyes wide in terror.

"What business do you have here?" I call out to the strangers.

The bearded man closest to me takes a step closer. "Shut your mouth, whore, or I will shut it for you."

Taken aback, Kristof is just about to attack him, when a taller bald man grabs the man. "We do not talk to women that way," he reminds the bearded man.

Anger flashes over his face, illuminated by the fire light. "She is traveling with men, what else would she be?"

"She would be our sister, sir, and you have insulted her honor. For those words, you will die," Kristof spits through his teeth. As the words leave his mouth an arrow plunges deep into the eye of the bearded man who insulted me.

The taller bald man lets Kristof go in surprise, and his biggest mistake was not disarming him. Kristof swings fast and low, disemboweling him all in one blow.

I race over to Laken, freeing him from his restraints.

"We need to pack up and move, there may be more of them," I order.

"As you wish, my queen," Kristof replies.

Laken walks over to help him with the tent as Thane emerges from the tree line, bow in hand.

I smile as he comes toward me. "That was a great shot. Next time whistle so I can take a step back."

Pulling me into his arms he says, "I would never hit you, my love."

"Even in the dark?"

He places his lips on mine as a reply. I enjoy the moment before we have to break apart.

When camp is torn down, we saddle the horses, and Thane extinguishes the fire. He then joins me on my horse and we head to Ravenwallow.

I lean back into Thane's strong arms, laying my head on his shoulder.

"Sleep, my queen. I will keep you safe, always," he whispers in my ear.

CHAPTER FOUR

*W*hen I wake I'm still on my horse, wrapped in the safety of Thane's arms. I peek back at him, and he peers down at me with a smile.

"Thank you for keeping me safe," I tell him.

"Always." That one word is all it takes to warm my heart.

I look ahead and I can see the town in the distance growing closer. It has been years since I have been here. The last time I recall I was just a little girl, my mother's last trip before her death.

The thought brings a tear to my eye. I wipe it away along with the memory. I have to find Evander; I must stay on task.

My focus turns to Kristof and Laken. They are swaying on their horses, and I can see their eyes fluttering and a head shake here and there.

Taking the reins from Thane, I urge our horse in front of the other two. We enter into the town slowly, heading straight for a tavern.

Thane dismounts. He turns and holds his arms for me to leap into them. I hand him the reins and hop down into his arms. His large hands grabs my waist. He pulls me to him and leans down for a kiss. I part my lips and his tongue enters my mouth. Only for a moment, just long enough to tease me and heat me to my core.

Saddened as he sets me down, I huff out, "You're a tease, you know that?"

He just winks as he ties the horse to the post. Kristof and Laken follow suit, but Kristof comes over and kisses me as well. He drapes an arm over my shoulder and we walk into the tavern.

Laken has a funny look on his face as he follows us.

I pause and turn to him. "What, did you want a kiss too?"

His cheeks flush as he shakes his head no.

Kristof turns me around as we head in. Thane goes straight to the bar making an arrangement for two rooms. As soon as he gets that squared away we head upstairs. Laken is deposited into his room, and he crashes as soon as his head hits the pillow.

The three of us enter our room and Kristof leads me to the bed, pulling me onto it with him. Kristof's body against the wall, my body next to him, and then Thane joins us.

"Rest for a little while, my queen. We will not be able to save Evander with no sleep," Kristof whispers in my ear.

Then he settles against the nape of my neck, lightly snoring in my ear.

Thane rolls over to face me. "Looking to finish what you started earlier?"

I raise an eyebrow at him. "As much as I'd love to, I'm trapped under Kristof's weight and I can barely keep my eyes open."

Thane kisses my forehead and nods. He closes his eyes and turns so that I can rest my head on his chest.

My fingers trail up and down under his shirt. Once I feel him relax under my touch, I clear my mind and wait for sleep to take me.

When I wake, I am surrounded by nothing but cold bedding. I jump out of bed, confusion taking over. It takes a moment before I realize where I am and why I am here, then my breathing returns to normal.

I walk to the wash basin and clean up. When I look in the mirror I catch sight of a gorgeous blue dress hanging on the back of the door.

I quickly strip and slide on the dress. The fabric is smooth to my touch and fits almost like a second skin. I step back in front of the mirror and let down my hair, running my fingers through the waves and untangling rat's nest. Once I am finally decent and presentable, I head down to find my men.

I spy them at the bar, taking notice that Laken has joined them and so have some barely dressed women. I approach just as one attempts to put her hands on Thane. Gripping her hand in mine I inch closer. I move the hair covering her ear and whisper, "These three are mine, please tell your friends the same."

As soon as I remove my hand, she steps away and so do her friends.

Laken raises an eyebrow at me and I just shrug in return.

"Maybe you were too pretty for them," I joke.

"That's definitely it," he says with a laugh.

"Okay boys, go chat up some of these men so we can find Evander," I order.

"What will you do, my queen?" Thane asks.

"Let them come to me." I smile.

I hear a rumble of laughter from each as they separate and head to the shadow filled corners of the tavern. I am not alone at the bar long when a very handsome stranger approaches me.

"How is it that a beautiful woman like you is here alone?" His voice is gruff and sexy all at once.

"I have been told I am too demanding," I tell him.

His mouth tips up into a smile. "In the bedroom or out?"

I thoughtfully tap my index finger on my chin and state, "Both."

This simply statement gets a rise of laughter from him. "What are you doing in a place like this? It doesn't seem like your kind of haunt."

I pull at my emotions, hoping to get my eyes to tear up. I look down at my almost empty glass, sadness filling my face as I raise it.

With tear filled eyes, I stare into his, and my voice breaks as I say, "I'm looking for my brother, Evander. He was taken by the mage, Lilthia."

He jumps back almost a foot, as if I threw acid at him. Fear then anger washes over his face. "You will not say that name in here again."

"Why are you angry with me? I answered your question," I meekly reply.

"She has plagued our village and kingdom for many years. She has taken up residence in the old Ramsay Manor on the hill. For your sake, do not attempt to rescue your brother. If she has taken him, he is dead already." He bids me goodbye.

I motion for Thane once the man is out of the tavern. Thane has to shake off another whore.

He smiles as he nears. "Sorry, that one was stubborn. As many times as I declined her company, I could not break free."

I look over and see she is still glaring at me. I move closer to Thane and then pull him into a kiss. He grips my hips and holds me to his body. Once I am satisfied, I move back an inch or two and look back to where she is standing.

If looks could kill I would be dead. She stomps up the stairs and out of sight.

Thane is laughing in my ear, and I pull out of his grip to face him. "What? I don't think she will be bothering you anymore. Back to the reason I called you over. I may have found her. Meet me upstairs in a few minutes. I'm going to rescue Kristof. He looks like he is playing cards in that corner, and we both know what a dreadful poker face he has."

I kiss Thane on the cheek and wait until I see him disappear up the stairs before slowly making my way over to Kristof. Once I'm standing behind his chair, I run my hands down his chest and whisper in is ear, "Upstairs, let's go."

I remove my hands from his chest, wink at the three men at the table.

I hear Kristof's chair slide on the wooden floor as he tells them, "Sorry fellas, I can't disappoint this beautiful lady. I'm out."

I hear their groans, and a smile crosses my face as I feel Kristof's arm wrap around my waist.

CHAPTER FIVE

Thane is sitting on the bed once Kristof and I enter the room.

"What did you find out, my queen?" Thane asks.

"A handsome stranger told me that Lilthia has been seen haunting a place called Ramsay Manor. That has to be where she's taken Evander. We must find where it's located and scout it out. I want to get Evander back as soon as possible. You two want to mingle some more? I would join you but this dress is riding up, and I can't wait to get out of it."

A smile crosses both of their faces; they look at each other then back to me. I have no chance to move before they both get their hands on me. I hear the tear of the fabric, and in a matter of seconds I'm only wearing my underwear.

Strips of what used to be my dress litter the wooden floor of the room. With my hands on my hips I glare at them.

"Now that you've had your fun, please pick up the fabric. Return downstairs and find where the manor is. Then come back and let's go get our boy," I order.

They comply and I walk to my pack and remove the outfit I had replaced earlier. I make my way back to the mirror, running a brush through my long locks before I braid them and pull it up. I don't want it to get caught or pulled when we go to save Evander. I slip my boots on and fasten my sword on my hip, ready and waiting my men's return.

After what seems like eternity, the door to the room flings open. I draw my sword but lower it only a little when I see that it is Laken who has come crashing in.

"Laken, you could've knocked first. What is the meaning of this?"

"My queen, some of the fine ladies of the house think you are stealing their men. We must make our leave before they come to harm you."

I can see the fear in his eyes and hear it in his tone, so I run to the bed for my pack, slinging it onto my shoulders as I take his hand. "Let's not delay, we need to get Thane and Kristof to the horses."

He follows, not trying to remove his hand from my grip as we descend the stairs at a blur's pace. Thane and Kristof see me holding Laken's hand, and a smile is plastered on Kristof's face while Thane wears a scowl. I ignore it as I motion for them to go outside. I almost reach the door before a well-endowed blonde is blocking the exit.

I smile sweetly. "Excuse me, I have to meet my friends outside."

Her scowl stays put and a husky voice exits her body as she responds. "My girls said you are hogging all the men. We don't put up with that here. If you come back, you won't be walking out without help."

"I won't darken your doorstep again," I assure her.

As soon as she moves, I dart out the door pulling Laken with me.

Thane and Kristof have the horses saddled and ready to go. I climb on and wait for Laken to join me.

"Thane, lead the way. Let us find Evander and get home," I command.

He turns his horse north, and I pull in line behind him with Kristof bringing up the rear.

Laken cautiously holds his hands on my hips, trying to keep his distance. He leans in just enough to whispers in my ear. "Why did you not put that woman in her place? You are her queen. She should not have talked to you that way. It made my blood boil with her disrespect."

I'm holding the reins, so I keep my eye forward even though I want to read his facial expression.

"There is a time and place to pull out the 'I am your queen' card. That was not it. We are out here looking for Evander, not to spat with my subjects. We must rid the kingdom of Lilthia and her reign of terror. She has had her time. She tortured my father, and then moved on to me. I have had to fight to rule, and I will fight for my people and rid them of her evil. Her taking Evander is the final straw."

He leans back and remains quiet. For the rest of the ride, there is no chatter. We keep our eyes open for any trouble.

Each step the horse takes the dirt becomes darker and the grass turns a muddier color. The trees have less leaves and have rot covering them. I know we are on the right path. Lilthia destroys and this dying vegetation confirms it.

My fear for Evander's safety is pulled to the front of my mind. A lump rises in my throat as the manor looms ahead of us.

Thane slows his horse down just enough for mine to meet up with his. We stop as Kristof joins us.

"What is the plan my queen?" Kristof asks.

"We will scout the area, find the best route in, and save Evander."

We tie our horses to a few of the closer trees. We also leave our packs, only taking our weapons with us. As we close in on the manor, I take my sword in hand. I have no idea what horrors Lilthia will have instore for us.

We are just a step from the back of the manor when I notice that Laken is no longer at my side.

As quietly as I can I whisper to Thane and Kristof, "Where did Laken go?"

They shrug and keep moving. My adrenaline is pumping now; he couldn't just disappear. We quicken our pace as the sun starts its descent for the night. Since splitting up is not an option we agree that the back door is where we should start the attack.

Thane takes the lead and Kristof follows me in. We have some daylight rays coming through the windows, so we aren't in complete darkness.

We enter what looks to be a kitchen and are greeted by stairs as we move into the next room.

"Let's go clear the top floor, then this floor and the cellar if we don't find Evander first. Keep an eye peeled for Laken, he may be in trouble too."

They nod in agreement and we start our ascent. Each step creaks under the weight of our feet, even when we step lightly to the next. Each noise seems to echo in the enclosed staircase; so much for the element of surprise.

Thane hits the landing first, holding a hand back telling me to stop. We must have chosen wisely, and he is trying to protect me from whatever is in that hall. Instead of waiting I take his hand and join him there, Kristof only a step behind me.

On the opposite end in dim candle light I can just make out Laken's beautiful features.

A smile rises on his lips when he sees me. "You were too

trusting and kind, Rose. I was so close to you and thought of all the ways in which I could kill you."

I am baffled at his statement. I raise an eyebrow. "What do you mean, Laken? I have done nothing to wrong you. I took you in, fed you, and treated you like I would anyone in my kingdom."

A fiendish laugh escapes his smiling lips. "What if I told you there was no Laken?"

I let out a barely audible gasp as I finally realize what his words mean.

With one wave of his hand, Thane and Kristof go flying down the stairs. I look back for just a moment to make sure they are okay, but in the darkness I can't see much of anything.

Turning back to where Laken was standing, I see Lilthia in his place.

"You cannot save them. Once I am done with you, it will be their turn! I will feast on your bones and flesh for weeks. After which I will return to the castle a hero for defeating the evil mage that has plagued Stonehelm for centuries," she cackles.

"You will have to kill me first," I yell, as I charge towards her. When I get to where she was standing she is gone.

She materializes out of thin air, just behind me, kicking me in the butt. I stumble but right my footing.

"Are you fool enough to think you can defeat me?" she snarls.

"I will fight you until my last breath. My people with be rid of you once and for all," I nearly growl.

I slash my blade, landing in on her arm. With a cry of pain, she steps back from me but raises her sword to strike.

Her blow lands heavily on my blade; I blocked her blow, her sword clashing hard on mine. I push with all my might and her sword is forced away. Lilthia stumbles back. Anger is written all over her face, and she charges toward me, her hands covered in blue flames. She extends them toward me and tries to burn me with them.

I dart to the side and she falls down the stairs. As she grips for something to slow her fall, she lights the rug on the stairs ablaze. I rush after her, careful to mind the flames. When she tries to stand, at the same time Thane and Kristof wrap their arms around her. She struggles to throw them off. I can see the electricity she is sending out in waves to my men. They flinch a little but hold on tight.

As I reach her, I ram my sword into her chest and through her heart. The moment my sword pierces it, she begins to writhe and turn to ash.

Once I remove my sword, she explodes in cloud of ash. The three of us cough and spit out what coats our mouths.

"Come, let us find Evander and head home," I choke out. "This place is about to go up in flames.

"I agree. Plus, this place gives me the creeps," Kristof replies.

I lead the way back upstairs, each of us spreading out and opening a door in our search. There are six doors on this floor alone. As we get to the last set, I push on the one in front of me and there, on a worn out wooden bed in the moonlight, is my sweet Evander.

I can see the rhythm of his chest moving up and down. He starts to toss and turn like I have watched so many nights as the nightmares overwhelm him. She did the worst torture imaginable to him, trapping him in his dreams.

I cross this weathered, wooden floor and approach him on the ratty bed he is lying on. The linens, even in this light, look like they haven't been cleaned in years, and there are holes where the mice have chewed them.

As I reach him, I can see the sweat beading upon his forehead. I sit down next to him and try and wake him. Gently shaking him, I whisper his name, then say it louder. None of it works. I look back to the doorway where Thane and Kristof are standing. They both shrug their shoulders, unsure what else to do.

I turn back to Evander and run my fingers through his white-blond hair.

"It is time to wake, my sleeping beauty," I whisper as I press my lips to his.

I sit back up and wait, a tear trailing down my cheek. A moment later I see his eyes flutter. Then they open and Evander is staring up at me with a smile on his face.

As he sits up, I grab him and tug him into my arms. "Oh Evander, I've missed you. We came as soon as could. I'm so sorry she took you. Her reign of terror is over."

He pulls back just enough to look me in the eyes. "I always knew you would come for me. I never doubted it."

"Let us get out of this creepy manor. Lilthia set it ablaze, so we must hurry. We will have to find a place to stay for the night. Long story, but we can't stay at the tavern in Ravenwillow," I say as we stand.

He takes my hand. "Well, we have a long ride ahead of us, and you'll have plenty time to fill me in."

ALSO BY JENEE ROBINSON

The Creeper Saga

Fate of the Fate

Curse of the Fae

Redemption of the Fae

Couldn't Keep Her

For Melissa Anthology

Typical Hunter Day

ABOUT THE AUTHOR

Jenée Robinson

Jenée Robinson
Jenée Robinson released her first novella, Fate of the Fae,
May 1st, 2018. She completed the trilogy on March 3, 2019.
She has completed several short stories, and has more
releasing soon. She is busy writing more, as well as more
novellas and books.
She is married and has three ornery girls.
Other than writing, she loves reading and photography.
She's a Harry Potter Nerd and loves the show Supernatural
and Captain America.

FOLLOW HER HERE:

Links to follow
FB Reader Group:
www.facebook.com/groups/faefulreaders

Bookbub:
www.bookbub.com/authors/jenee-robinson

facebook.com/jeneerobinsonauthor
twitter.com/jeneer82
instagram.com/jeneerobinson82

ALWAYS DREAMING

By K.A. Morse

Heat Level- Sweet As Cherry Pie

NOTE FROM THE AUTHOR

This work is a fictitious story. The names, places, occurrences, companies, organizations and such are products of the Author's imaginations or have been used in a fictitious manner. They are not to be construed as real. Any resemblance to persons, living or dead, actual events, locations, companies, or organizations are purely coincidental. The authors do not assume the responsibility of the content on 3rd party websites. You can purchase a copy of this book at Amazon.com

This is to all the dreamers. Never give up on them!

CORA ANN

*a*s I sit in my room staring out the window into our rose garden, I daydream. The rain is coming down hard today so I dream from my room. Ever since I can remember, all I ever wanted to do was dream, but being a princess is not that easy. Always having to do the right thing, act the right way.

When I can sneak off and get a moment to myself, there are two places I can be found—our flower garden or the highest tower in our castle. These are the perfect places for me to daydream about being free of my duties as a princess, not having to please anyone, or be ladylike if I didn't want to. Whether it is dragons to fight or magic carpets to fly on, my dreams are mine and no one can take them away from me.

When I hear the door open I turn to find my mother has come to see me. I'm sure she's wanting to talk to me about upcoming events. Without a word, I move to the vanity to have my hair brushed. One of our favorite things to do together.

"Cora Ann, Luke is very excited to meet you," my mother informs me.

With my eighteenth birthday fast approaching, I am to meet my betrothed for the first time. We have been engaged since I was born, but I didn't want to marry a stranger.

"Mother, why do I have to marry someone I haven't even met?" I ask, as she gently brushes my hair while we sit in my room.

"Why darling, your father promised you to King James's son, Luke, the day you were born. It cannot be changed. I have done all that I can to change his mind, but it's simply not possible," my mother sets the brush onto the vanity in front of me and our eyes lock in the mirror, I can see a look of sadness on her face.

I turn to look at her. My beautiful mother has milky white skin and fiery red hair, which is pulled back into a braid that goes halfway down her back. .

"I've always been so jealous of your hair Mother. Why did I have to get this dull, brown color?" I confess, wanting to change the subject. I get up and move about my room feeling trapped and hoping the movement will help.

"You have your father's hair, my dear." Mother smiles at me. "I also have a surprise for you. I know you've been nervous about meeting your betrothed for the first time, so we decided that for your birthday we will have a huge ball, and you will meet your intended," she informs me.

Every muscle in my body tightens.

My mother continues talking, as if unaware of my turmoil. "We have the most beautiful dress being made for you! I can't wait to see you in it, my darling daughter." She stands and glides toward the door, but turns back, waiting for my response.

"Thank you. I can't wait for the party." The fakest smile I can possibly make is plastered on my face, when all I want to do is throw myself on my bed and cry. "I can't wait to see my dress Mother. I'm sure it will be perfect."

When she leaves the room, the tears begin streaming down my face. I don't want to meet Luke, because meeting him will make my future *real*.

The thought of marrying a complete stranger is something that I never wanted. I've told my father my feelings, but to no avail. My dreams and daydreams are now my only escape.

I plop myself on my bed until my tears dry. When I look back up, my fairy godmother, Gabriella, is sitting on the edge of my bed. I'm so thankful to see her. It isn't often she drops by, but when she does, she's always the perfect shoulder to cry on. And even though her magic can fix many things for me, it's usually her advice I find more valuable than her magic.

"Oh precious, what is the matter?" The older woman is only four feet tall, but she crosses the room with the fierceness of a giant, and wipes away the last of my tears with her gentle touch.

I take a deep breath, "Tomorrow I'm going to have to meet my betrothed. I don't think I can be with someone I don't know or love," I explain to her. "Is there anything you can do to help me?"

"My dear, I don't quite know what you want me to do. This is the path that is chosen for you," Gabbie says as her brow furrows with thought.

"All I want to do is sleep forever, so I can dream and not live the nightmare of an arranged marriage," I plead. "This is very unbecoming of a princess, but I just can't go through with a marriage that is not based on love. Please?" I hate how whiny I sound. "I know it's my party but the wedding will be shortly after."

A smile spreads across Gabbie's face. "Well, my dearest, I may be able to do something for you, but the magic comes at a price. Not a bad price, per se, but a price nonetheless. I can put you to sleep, but the only way to be awoken is with true love's kiss."

I pause. Perhaps I should be scared of magic and of the price involved, but I'm not. If there's one curse I can handle, it's one where I sleep. And the idea of getting my true love in the end of it? Well, it's everything I've ever wanted and more.

"Yes, Gabbie, please. If it's true love waking me up, this is something I can handle," I agree, hope blossoming within me.

This is the happiest I've ever felt. Finally, something for me! My parents can't control this part of my life. At last I will be at one with my dreams and the only way I'll awaken is by true love. I may not know him, but at least I'll know it's meant to be. Gabbie hasn't told me when the magic will happen. Until then, I will have to bide my time.

Today is the day of my eighteenth birthday and waking up is dreadful. I haven't seen Gabbie since the night she promised me she would let me dream. I lock myself away in my room, pacing the floor, hoping Gabbie will finally show up. The hours until the party tick by, quickly approaching the allotted time.

A knock at the door makes me jump. Gabbie wouldn't use the door, so I already know who it is, and I know I can't do anything to reveal my plans to escape the ball or my arranged marriage. Going to the door, I promptly open it and paste a smile on my face.

My mother is there with two of her maids, Adeline and Kea. Adeline is holding a beautiful dark blue dress in her hands. I let them in and feel a little guilty. They're here to prepare me for the ball tonight. A ball I have no intention of attending.

When I undress, Adeline and Kea help me into my new gown and Kea zips me in. I look down at the stunning sapphire blue dress that fits me like a glove. The princess cut style accentuates my body, without straps marring its lines, and the fabric falls in a cascade, with a small flare at the bottom. The dress is silky to the touch and soft on my skin. I don't know how my mom got it to fit like this, but it is perfect. I run my hands along the light blue jewels that encrust the sweetheart neckline where it dips in to show off my breasts.

It's strange. This gown is so beautiful, and yet it fills me with nothing but sadness. My parents want so badly for me to look nice for the prince tonight, and all I want is to escape.

Adeline follows me as I sit in front of the vanity. As soon as I am settled, she begins her work on my makeup, while Kea works on my hair. By the time the two of them are done, I don't even recognize myself. I feel so beautiful, unlike I ever have before. Mother has outdone herself.

And then my smile falters, all I can picture is me asleep. At least if it's going to happen, I'll look nice when it does. The thought should reassure me, but I only feel guilty that all my mother's hard work will be wasted.

"Alright, darling, we will let you know when it is time to announce you. Guests should be starting to arrive soon. I need to be there to greet them with your father. We would like you to be a surprise, as you haven't met your intended yet." My mother smiles as she leaves, with Kea and Adeline quickly following behind her.

Feeling deflated, I'm left alone once again to pace the floor. As I turn around to look out my window, Gabbie stands face to face with me. I let out a yelp.

"Gabbie, where have you been?" I ask, desperation seeping into my tone. I hate hearing that in my own voice.

"Sorry, Cora Ann. For magic this strong, I had to take my

time to make it just right. You cannot rush it. Something could go terribly wrong. And I do love you honey," Gabbie explains to me as she's holding a small vile. "I want you to wake once your true love is found. So all you have to do is drink this and you shall sleep and dream." She hands me the vile and with a soft, "Sweet Dreams," she is gone.

I amble to my bed and sit with the little bottle still in my hand. Contemplation is key. Do I really want to do this? Am I being too selfish and only thinking of myself right now? Before I can change my mind, I gulp down the potion, then I lay down and close my eyes.

QUEEN JOAN

*I*t's time for Cora Ann's grand entrance. I send Adeline to retrieve her. A couple of minutes later Adeline returns, rushing to my side, but I don't see Cora Ann preparing to come down the stairs for her presentation.

"My Queen, there's something wrong with the princess. I can not get her to wake," Adeline says with worry on her face.

I rise from my seat and rush to my daughter's room. I slam her door open and there she lies, still as can be. I go to her and attempt to wake her but she does not stir as I shake her, and tears begin rolling down my cheeks.

What if she is not sleeping and has died somehow?

I kneel next to her and continue to cry. I am startled as a hand touches my shoulder. When I look up, my eyes land on Gabriella.

"Do not fret my Queen. She can be awakened, but only by true love's kiss," Gabriella explains, as tears still stream down my face.

"Why has this happened Gabriella?" I inquire as I stand

and dry my tears. I take a seat on the bed next to my daughter.

"My Queen, this was her birthday wish from me. I could not deny Cora Ann her request." Gabriella's confession is not making it any easier to take in what has happened.

"Strange men need to come into my daughter's room and kiss her to see if they are her true love? I'm not sure I like the sound of this," I tell her, as I look to Cora Ann. She lies there peacefully and looks so happy in this sleep. "So what do I tell all the guests who have come to see my daughter for this party?"

"My Queen, tell them she has fallen ill and cannot attend," she states, and then disappears as fast as she came.

She's given me a lot to think about and I still must tell my husband, the king. He is not going to be happy with any of this. I must leave my daughter and tend to other things before I can return to her.

CORA ANN

6 Months Asleep

I come across a small village that looks like it's under attack. I glance down and am dressed for battle with my silver armor, and my brown hair pulled back and braided. I set off into town to see what all the commotion is about. As I get closer, I notice a few of the houses to the left are on fire. Villagers are crying and screaming at the men setting the village aflame. As I watch, a couple of knights drag a family from their home, then set fire to it. The children are clinging to their mother's legs, screaming. I run to free the woman from the men's clutches. I come upon the first man, hitting him from behind with the hilt of my of my sword. He goes down quickly, the stupid oaf should have had his helmet on. The second one quickly turns toward me with his sword pulled out. He swings it at me, but I block it with mine. I push forward, throwing him off balance and to the ground. He wasn't expecting me to be as strong as I am. Once I see an opening in his defense, I take my shot, stabbing him in the side. Not a fatal wound, but enough to keep him down. He won't be pillaging this town anymore. I move on, deeper into the village.

Why the heck don't I have a horse to ride? I can't move fast enough.

All of a sudden I'm on a horse, galloping toward the center of the village. I have an army behind me who are dressed in the same armor I am. I yell, "Charge!" and I see the fear in the invaders' eyes as we get closer and closer. We start pushing them back to the outskirts of town. Once I have them where I want them, I dismount my horse and begin combat.

I unsheathe my sword heading for the first man down the hill in my way. He looks up at me with surprise in his eyes as I bring my sword down upon his head. My blade connects with his neck as he tries to dodge my blow. Blood comes pouring out of his wound, spraying all over me.

One down, so many more to go.

My men have made it to me and are thick in the fight as well. I'm dodging arrows and swords. The fighting feels like it has gone on for hours and I'm starting to become fatigued. I sense that I have reached my limit, my arms are starting to feel like jello. Just as I bring my sword down again, I look up and I'm the last one standing. Covered in blood, I stand as the wind blows my brown hair behind me as the blood of the man I just killed trickles from my hand. Suddenly, I'm kissing a handsome man in fine, expensive looking clothes as if he's a prince or something. I quickly pull away from him.

"I'm sorry, who are you and why are we kissing?" I ask him harshly, as I try to look presentable.

Who am I kidding, I'm covered in blood, there's no helping my appearance now. There is something about him that is pulling me toward him, with his dark brown hair and hazel eyes. He has a delicious square jawline and full, pouty lips. The tightness of his clothes makes me think he had muscles trying to escape the confines of the fabric. I want that kiss again, to feel the warmth of his body close to mine. He speaks, bringing me out of my head and back to him.

"I am Prince Rodrick of Azua. I have traveled far to find out if I am the true love of Princess Cora Ann. I leaned down and kissed her... uh, well you. Then I found myself here, still kissing you. So have you awakened?" he inquires promptly, giving me a huge smile.

"I'm so sorry Rodrick, but if I'm still dressed like this then we are most definitely not awake. So how many princes have tried to wake me, do you know?" I question him as I circle him to size him up. "Are you the first, or just one of many?"

He gives me a puzzled look. "How long do you think you've been asleep?"

"Honestly, I don't know. I don't age in my dreams so it could be years or it could be days." I put my hand to my mouth as I consider the thought. "Tell me now, how long have I been asleep?"

CORA ANN

2 Years Asleep

*T*he first day we met he never did answer any of my questions. Just left me to wonder. I cannot shake Prince Rodrick. No matter how many times my dreams change, and I with them, he's always right there with me. He is really starting to bother me. In my dreams I can do anything I want, but he is the one thing I can't control. It's like he is controlling the dream as well. This, I am not okay with. I asked Gabbie to put me to sleep so I could get away from princes I didn't know.

"Come along Rodrick! We will never get to the top of this mountain with you moving so slowly," I call back to him, as I keep trekking up to the top, my faithful walking stick in hand.

I swear I hear him huff behind me, making me giggle. He's been a stick in the mud on every adventure we've been through. As I keep my pace I feel a pull on the rope. Looking back, I see that Rodrick has fallen into the snow and is about to bring me down with him. I run to him, helping him up.

"Oh, my poor Rodrick, you don't care for snow, do you?" I

ask him as I extend my hand to help him up before we both start to fall down the distance we have scaled.

"For the heavens, no. And who would want to do this for fun?" he retorts, as he pushes my hand away, too proud for my assistance.

"Fine, once we are done with this journey, you can pick our next adventure," I offer with a scowl.

Once he's back up I take the lead again. What a jerk to dismiss my hand like that.

I hope he gets eaten by a Yeti.

A giggle escapes my lips. I keep my head down and pull my coat tighter to fight off the wind and the sting of the cold. How can I feel the cold even in a dream? Must have something to do with the magic of the potion. I haven't seen any shelter the whole way up. When we are about ten feet from the top, I see it—a cave. The hole is huge, and I feel the urge to go inside. I know I shouldn't, but I slowly make my way to it. There's a torch waiting for me to grab once I hit the entrance. I hear Rodrick behind me, yelling for me not to enter.

I roll my eyes as I grab the light source with my free hand. We wouldn't be able to see in the cave without it when all I see is blackness, even with the torch in hand. Still, I push on. Rodrick is now pulling on the rope that has us tethered together. I wave the fire at him, making him stop.

"Could you stop?" I yell. "We are going in there whether you like it or not!"

"Why do we have to go into a place like this? We don't know what could be lurking in the darkness," he cautions with fear in his eyes.

"Oh, come on! Where's your sense of adventure?" I ask, as I turn back around and start in again.

This time he doesn't fight me. I lead the way, like always. I'm so glad he's not my true love because I couldn't handle him being this wimpy. I need someone who's going to be brave and fight alongside me. Better yet, a man who will fight for me to the end. No questions asked. That's what true love is, isn't it? Wow, I'm in my head now, back to the task at hand —seeing what's in the cave.

It mostly looks like a cave and nothing seems out of place. As I go farther, I feel a crunch under my feet. I bring the fire down so I can see why, and let out a short scream. All I see are bones everywhere. There is a strange growl behind us. I whip around and see a yeti standing on the path, blocking our way out. Fear falls across my face, but I don't scream. I do hear Rodrick shriek though. I so want to laugh but fear has me in its grips right now.

Rodrick takes charge, and unties himself from me. He lets out a battle cry and runs at the yeti. As he tackles the creature, he yells at me to get out of the cave. I've never seen him so assertive. This is a new side and I like it. Why hasn't he shown this side of himself before? There is an appealing strength about him, but now isn't the time to dwell on it. I skirt around them and run until I can't get my breath, but never looking back. I've found myself at the top of the mountain alone, cold, and scared out of my mind. The only weapon I have is my walking stick, since I dropped the torch while I was running for my life. At the peak, I find a rock to sit on. Tears are starting to form in my eyes as I see movement in the snow. I look up to see Rodrick. The waterworks come and I sag in relief that he's survived. I run to him, throwing my arms around his neck. I guess he's grown on me more than I knew.

"I can't breathe," Rodrick says, lightly gasping for air.

As I let go we are no longer on the top of the mountain. All I see are blue skies and water everywhere. I am dressed in almost nothing, with only two pieces of cloth covering my breasts and other private parts. I quickly search for a place to hide or something to cover up with. All Rodrick can do is laugh at me as I hastily move about, trying to hide myself. I see something that looks like a rock and chuck it at his head. Of course, I miss. He only laughs harder at me.

"How did you bring us here? Really, this is your adventure? To get me half naked on the beach?" I remark with a scowl on my face.

"Naked would have been better." He grins as he turns and makes his way to the ocean in only his undergarments.

"I do like my view from here," I mumble, as I take his backside in. I never knew he had markings on his back.

For a prince, I was also very surprised to see all the scars he wore. It looks like he hasn't had an easy life. What kind of prince gets beatings that leave scars like that? My mind is reeling with so many questions, no wonder he has taken so long to open up. Someone has hurt this poor soul terribly. Making my way to the water, I zoom past Rodrick, splashing him in the process. A grin spreads across my face, since I've never been in the ocean before and all of this is new to me. The waves start crashing into my body as two strong arms cradle me. I look up to find Rodrick smirking down at me.

"Let me go," I demand, as he drops me into the water.

I struggle to come back up from the water's depths, but it's all in vain. The pain in my lungs grows stronger as I fight for my breath. Out of nowhere a hand grabs my arm, pulling me up. Rodrick's eyes are wide with fear and water comes flying out of my mouth, hitting him in the face. A laugh wants to escape, but I'm too busy coughing up the water that went down my throat. Once the water has left my lungs, we head back to shore.

"I have found that the ocean is not my friend." My voice comes out hoarse.

All he can do is laugh at my words as we sit down in the sand. One of his arms slowly slides around my shoulders when the shivers set in. The cool breeze has put a chill in my bones.

"Something to cover up with would be nice, or a fire would be wonderful—with some food. Food sounds great. When is the last time we've eaten anything?" I ask, turning to look him in the eyes.

He gives me a grunt then gets up to go look for some wood. This puts a smile on my face. A girl could get used to bossing such a hot guy around.

Could he be my true love? If he is, why wasn't I awakened when he kissed me?

I hop up to see what Rodrick is doing, and I find him a good distance down the beach, heading toward me with an armful of timber and humming a tune. A smile starts to form on my face when suddenly, there's a new man kissing me. I pull away as fast as possible.

"Who are you?" I demand.

QUEEN JOAN

"*G*abbie what is going on?" I plead with her, not understanding why Cora Ann won't wake.

"Honestly, I don't know my Queen, she should have awaken after Rodrick kissed her. I felt for sure that he was the one." Her face is puzzled as she looks at the new prince that fell asleep.

"Prince Mason will be moved next to Prince Rodrick. They will be tended to until they awaken," I state, having remained at my daughter's side for the last two years.

My husband, the king, has been scouring the lands in search of princes to see if one could wake Cora Ann. With her twenty first birthday quickly approaching, we have high hopes she will be awake so we can celebrate it with her. Two of the princes have now fallen into the deep sleep our Cora Ann is under, and this worries me. How do we explain to Mason's parents what's wrong with him? It was hard enough with Rodrick's mother. All they did was kiss her. The princes have been put in a room together. Their beds are close to windows so the sun's rays can touch them off and on throughout the day. Rodrick's mother has not left him, except to sleep herself, since he fell asleep. For a queen, something felt different about her. Queen Marie didn't hold herself the same way as the other royals I have met do. The clothes she wears appear dated, but I hold my tongue since her son is now under this spell. Marie is one I make sure to keep a close eye on.

"All we can do is wait and hope the king can find the right prince to wake our princess. I'm so sorry I have done this." Gabbie's face hangs with regret as she says this. "I had hoped that a prince would be found rather quickly."

With that Gabbie is gone, leaving me with Cora Ann.

CORA ANN

"Well princess, I'm Prince Mason of Vestan. It is nice to kiss... meet you," he introduces himself, with a smile adorning his handsome face.

Mason looks very different than Rodrick. As I untangle myself from Mason's arms, Rodrick is upon us and not happy to see our company.

"A bit overdressed for the beach, aren't you?" Rodrick frowns, stepping closer to me as if claiming me as his own.

"Well, lets just fix that." I smile and we are swept away to a tavern.

We are all in proper clothing now. The guys might be dressed in a bit tighter clothing than their liking, but I'm sure enjoying the view. I snicker as drinks are brought to our table. Rodrick ensures he's next to me so he can stare down Mason. I take him in as well, from his shoulder length blond hair, to his sea blue eyes that I could get lost in all day. His nose is a bit wide and crooked, but Mason's lips are really the only thing off about him. His top lip is a thin line, while the bottom is pretty full and pouty. An elbow hits me in the ribs, bringing me back to reality.

"What was that for?" I snap at him, as the wench comes with more drinks.

"Your food will be out shortly," she declares promptly, then walks away.

We all grab a mug, taking a big gulp. I want to spit mine out, but I swallow it down instead, not wanting to look weak in front of them, but this was the most vile thing that I've ever tasted. Rodrick and Mason seem to have no problem drinking whatever this stuff is. I try not to make any faces but they are both laughing at me, so that must not have worked. About the time I'm going to open my mouth to yell at them, our food appears. The wench seems all too happy to serve Mason his plate of turkey and potatoes, sparing Rodrick and I just a glance as she sets ours down. Her breasts are almost hanging out as she's serving him, but if she bends over they will come out for sure.

Wow Cora Ann, this is your dream, what is going on? Why can't you control what is happening anymore?

"Miss, he's fine, thanks for the help," I dismiss her quickly. I can hear the jealousy in my voice.

Where did that come from? Normally men are throwing themselves at me, so to have Mason's eye on someone else is surprising. I shake it off, turning my attention to the food in front of me. The fork is nowhere to be seen so I just dig in with my fingers. Rodrick picks up the potato wedge with his hand and eats it, as does Mason. The change is strange but nice. Once done eating my hands are greasy from the turkey leg. There are no napkins, so I look to the guys to see what to do to clean my hands. They both wipe their hands on their pants, so I use Rodrick's pants too. Why get mine dirty? Rodrick's eyes are wide with surprise when I do this. The smile that spreads across my face as I do this seems to make him at a loss for words.

"No sense in my clothes getting all greasy too," I remark,

grinning from ear to ear with a twinkle in my eyes. "So what should our next adventure be?" My face is beaming with excitement.

Rodrick huffs. "Haven't we done it all? We've been on a million adventures. How long have we been at this?"

"Two years," Mason chimes in, making us both turn to him as our jaws almost hit the floor. "Well, two and a half for you, Cora Ann, when I tried kissing you. Who knows how long has passed in your dream world since then." He doesn't sound too hopeful about any of this.

"Wow, I've missed my nineteenth and twentieth birthdays. So my twenty-first is approaching. I do miss my mom and the warmth of her hugs," I gasp out before I begin to sob uncontrollably.

Two strong arms wrap around me. Not fighting it, I let the tears come as I lean into Rodrick's chest. Once my pity party's over, I wipe away what tears remain and remember this is of my own making. So I'm going to make the most of it. Finally free of Rodrick's arms, it's now time to set out on a new quest.

"Who wants to slay a dragon?" The wickedness in my smile takes them aback.

Rodrick and Mason give each other a glance then look back at me, their eyes wide with what I'm hoping is excitement.

I get up quickly and make my way to the door, not waiting for them. What wonders awaits us? My men grab each of my hands as we walk out of the door, not wanting to be left behind. Finally free of their grips, we walk down the path looking at this village. It looks a lot like my home. The memories and smells of home come flooding in, but I hold back the tears. In the dream realm this pain shouldn't be felt, since I don't care to feel it. I shake the thought from my head and go on to find me a dragon. We go to a couple shops, talking to the people to see if they have heard of any dragons close by, or if we need to travel. They all look at us like we have lost our minds. As we step foot out of another tavern, a huge black dragon with golden scales flies overhead. It releases its fire upon the town. The townspeople come out of the burning buildings screaming while holding their children.

Rodrick turns to me. "Well, you wanted a dragon, you got a huge one. Not sure how we are going to kill it, or even get to it."

"First, I know we need some armor and swords," Mason remarks with a toothy smile on his face.

"By golly, you are in luck! The next place we are going is the blacksmith's. Besides swords, I bet we can find something there. If not, they can point us in the right direction." I wink at them and I start toward the building, skipping along the way.

The blacksmith has nothing for us. We must go to the castle to get anything we need. I scratch my head in disbelief as he tells us all the weapons are stored there. The townspeople are not allowed to have artillery of any kind in the village. It's all to be kept in the castle and used by the guards. This set me aback. How can they protect themselves from thieves when the knights aren't about? I told the blacksmith thank you and set my sights on the castle. There is no sign of the dragon, so we don't have to hide as we make our way toward the looming structure. It's a straight shot up the middle of the village . Rodrick and Mason try their best to walk in front of me, but I refuse to let that happen. This is my mission, and they will not put me in the shadows.

The trek to the castle is a bit farther than expected, and since my belly is still full from our meal, it feels about ready to come back up. I bend over for a moment to catch my breath and both my guys rush to my side.

"Cora Ann, are you okay?" Mason asks, as he squats down next to me.

I sit on the ground with my back against the wall that surrounds the castle, under the shade of a tree. "Yes. This dress was not made for this heat, more for cold weather. So my food is wanting to make a reappearance. Give me a bit under this tree and I should be fine," I explain, flashing a weak smile at both of them to ease their worry.

Once my strength has returned, I hop up and give them both a mischievous grin. "Come on you lazy bums, we have a dragon to kill."

Back to myself, we walk to the main gates. Two knights block our path, barring our entrance. I try my best to sweet talk them, but they aren't buying what I'm trying to sell. The knights' faces don't change at all, they don't even look at me. They continue looking over my head in fact.

"Well you aren't very polite guards, now are you boys?" I ask them, batting my eyes and hoping that will work on them.

Still nothing, I place my hands on my hips and try to think of how to get past them. Rodrick and Mason step up to try their luck, or so I thought. They both pull back and hit the knights in the face, knocking them to the ground.

"Cora Ann, this is our chance, now run!" Mason insists, as he takes off through the main gate.

Rodrick and I are quick to follow him, running toward the castle entrance. As I look back, the guards are now up and chasing us, also screaming for us to stop. When we make it to the opening, we are stopped by another set of knights. My eyes roll when I see them. *Can't I catch just one break?* This dream just isn't going as easy as the others. Maybe Mason is fighting the magic that has brought us all here.

The knights take us in front of the king. Hopefully the king will listen to why we have come.

All the king says is one word: "Speak."

I step forward to address him, but before I can get the words out I hear a voice behind me.

"Oh father I heard we had visitors. Well, I mean people trying to break into the palace." A beautiful young lady walks in, taking a seat next to the king.

"Your majesties, we have come to kill the dragon that plagues the village. All we ask is for armor and swords," Rodrick states, moving in front of Mason and me.

The princess's face lights up as Rodrick gets closer to them. This makes me want to snatch his hand and hold it so she knows that he's mine. I refrain from doing so as Rodrick is making some headway with the princess. She keeps laughing and batting her eyes at his every word. By the time his lips stop moving, she's practically on top of him and leaning in for a kiss. This is something I can no longer handle and I step between them with a smile. The princess seems less than pleased by this as she hisses, "What is the meaning of this?" She glares at me, her eyes like daggers.

"We are only here for the dragon, your highness. Nothing more," I tell her with the biggest fake smile I can possibly manage.

"That's enough," the king finally speaks. "What makes you sure you can defeat this dragon? None of my men could." His face is stern as he waits for an answer.

Mason now takes his turn to talk. "This is what we do. We go from kingdom to kingdom getting rid of their problems. Just last week we slayed a troll that lived under a bridge," he lies with no hesitation in his voice.

The king now waves his hand. "Fine, you can have what you need. But don't come back until the dragon is dead or you will be killed."

We all agree to his terms and are taken to the armory. My eyes are wide with wonder at all the armor and swords they have. Mason is the first to be fitted for his armor, followed by Rodrick. When it's my turn they just laugh.

"I am a dragon slayer too, so I suggest you find me something and get those smiles off your smug faces, or I will take them off," I warn with a wink and smile.

The knights scurry to find something to fit me. They almost look worried since they can't find anything that is my size. Finally, they find a set of armor in the corner and come rushing to me with smiles on their faces. The set they found looks like that of a teenager, but it's the perfect fit for me. We are given swords and shields, then told where the dragon lives.

"You could have given us a ride. You know, a horse or three," I yell as they leave us back at the entrance.

"Well, if we start now we should be there by nightfall," Rodrick informs us, so we start our long trek to the dragon's lair. Sunset here is just as beautiful as it is at home. I didn't even feel the tears until Mason reaches over and wipes one away.

"Missing home more than I thought I was," I explain, brushing away the other tears.

"Hopefully we will all wake soon and you will be home again," Mason reassures me with a grin.

"But then I awake to what? Two soulmates or more? What then?" I ask him, with uncertainty all over my face.

Rodrick comes from behind and hushes us, pointing to the woods before us. Well, there's not much left of it. Our pace slows as we approach the mountain entrance. Sounds of something like snoring are coming from inside, but we can see bursts of fire shooting from the opening.

"I think the dragon is asleep," Mason says.

Rodrick and I both look at him with our heads tilted to the side, wondering if he really just said that.

In a hushed voice I murmur, "Let's be as quiet as possible. That way maybe we can sneak up on him."

Slowly, we keep walking toward the bursts of flames. As we hit the entrance, there lies the dragon. It's so much bigger and beautiful up close. How could we kill such a wondrous creature? I'm having second thoughts about this, but Rodrick and Mason are already charging for the dragon. Those idiots let out what I'm guessing are their battle cries as they run. The dragon's eyes pop open and it starts to stir. They are just about to reach the dragon when they both disappear.

Abruptly, I'm waking up to a man kissing me. This one I haven't seen previously, but before I can say anything, my mother comes rushing to my side. Tears fill her eyes as she grabs me, hugging me, before I can try and get up. Once she lets me go, all I want to do is move and stretch my legs. It isn't easy standing for the first time, since my limbs aren't wanting to listen to my brain, and I almost fall to the ground once as I try to stand. The strange man is right there to catch me. As he's helping me onto my bed, Kea comes rushing into the room.

"Your majesty, the other two have—" She stops mid sentence when she sees I'm awake and comes running to me. "I'm so glad you are awake princess."

I embrace her and whisper a thank you since my throat is dry. She can tell and hurries to the nightstand to grab me some water.

"Kea, what were you going on about?" my mother inquires, as she come back to me with the glass.

"The princes have woken up!" Kea squeals, then dismisses herself.

The water helps my throat, and I am able to speak. "Are their names Rodrick and Mason?" I question my mother, who is sitting next to me on the bed.

"Cora Ann, how did you know their names?" Her face is looking at me with surprise.

"We've been on many adventures together in my dreams," I reply with a smile, now turning to the prince who woke me. "Can you please help me to the other princes? Prince…"

"Jordan. Prince Jordan." His voice is low and raspy. His dirty blond hair falling in front of his green eyes. "And yes I can."

Jordan helps me up, and we make our way down the hall to the room that holds Mason and Rodrick. At the entrance I pause. What if they don't feel the same way I do? Now Jordan's in the mix, how will they feel that I have more than one true love? So many questions are running through my mind. As soon as Mason's eyes meet mine, he is up and out of bed, ignoring who I'm guessing is his mother, to come see me. His embrace is bittersweet. He had grown on me in our shared dreamland. Once he lets go of me, my eyes search for Rodrick. He is sitting up on his bed, just as weak as I am. We were in the dream world the longest. It's like Jordan knows what I want, helping me over to Rodrick. I sit down next to him, and he wraps his arms around me like he has so many times before in my dreams.

"We're home," I whisper to him as I cry into his chest.

RODRICK

One Week Later

*O*nce I've regained my full strength, I travel home to grab some mementos I can't leave behind. My heart hurts being so far from Cora Ann. I knew I loved her from the moment I saw her, even though she's so strong minded. To leave my mother and sister is hard, but they know it is needed so I can free them from the evil mistress that runs the house we all work for. Once I'm done gathering my things, I say goodbye to my mother and Airabella.

"Bella, take care of mother until I can come for you both, please," I plead, already knowing she will. "I will come for you as soon as I can, I promise."

As I turn to leave, my mother stops me and hands me a beautiful suit, fit for a prince. I withhold my tears back as I take if from her, and return to Cora Ann's kingdom. By horse it's only half a day's ride, as I am in the next kingdom ruled by King James. Nightfall is upon me when I reached Ashburn. Cora Ann greets me at the main gate. Mason and Jordan aren't far behind her. I dismount my horse and smile at her. Happy to be with her again, not even minding that I have to share her with the other two.

"So glad you are back," she says with a playful smirk.

"What do you have up your sleeve?" I reply, giving her a quick kiss on the forehead.

"We've been invited to a ball in honor of Prince Luke's twenty-third birthday celebration. Plus, since he wasn't one of my true love's, they are inviting all eligible women between eighteen and twenty to attend as well. By the end of the night Luke must pick his wife," she explains to me.

"When is this happening?" I inquire with a puzzled look.

"Two days time," she answers. "Now put your horse away, dinner is getting cold," she orders, then walks away, Jordan and Mason right behind her.

After I take my horse to the stables, putting her up for the night, I make my way to the dining hall. Everyone is seated, waiting on me to join them so they can eat.

"I'm sorry. You didn't have to wait on me," I murmur quietly, as I take my seat across from Cora Ann.

"Nonsense Rodrick, you now live here and will marry my daughter soon. You will be treated no different than any royal in this room. We will all eat our supper together, as family," the queen explains to me.

She makes me feel more welcome than I have in a long time. A smile spreads across my face as the food is served.

The day of the ball is upon us. We are getting into coaches, the king and queen with us. The guys get in one that is also meant for the king. Cora Ann and her mother ride together. It's an awkward ride to the next kingdom as the king doesn't say a word to us, so we don't speak at all. Today I wear the outfit my mother gave me. She's always known how to make my clothes fit perfectly. Finally, we make it back to my home kingdom of Firestone. I pray no one remembers me while we are here. Even being Cora Ann's true love, the truth of my match isn't widely spread.

We pull up first. It's almost dusk when I step out of the coach. I can smell the rain coming, the scent is one of my favorites. I hope it holds off until we have left. As Cora Ann's carriage stops, I go to help her and the queen descend. They take my arm as they step out, both stunning in their gowns. They smile at me as they step down. The queen and king are arm in arm as they enter the castle. Cora Ann is walking in with Mason and Jordan, with me following behind. We enter the grand hall as they announce us. I snicker because ours is longer than everyone else's. There is dinner and dancing. We take turns dancing with our Cora Ann. Prince Luke does the same with all the single ladies that have come tonight. He has a big decision to make. I turn back to Cora Ann, so beautiful in her pink dress. As I watch her dance with Jordan, I notice everyone's eyes are going to the grand staircase.

A beautiful women is coming down the stairs in a light blue dress. A closer look at her, reveals she is my sister, Bella. My eyes get bigger. I want to run to her and give her a hug. We can't act like we know each other. She now has Prince Luke's attention as he's stopped dancing with a lady to go to Bella. I feel the urge to get to my sister first so I can protect her from him, not knowing how he would treat her. Once Luke reaches her, Bella smiles and lights up the whole room. Luke only has eyes for her. He whisks her off to the dance floor, and it's as if everyone else disappears for them. I lose track of the pair when he takes her to a different part of the castle.

"What are you thinking about?" Cora Ann asks me, breathless from dancing with Jordan.

"Just hoping this isn't a dream too," I tell her with a smile. "Why don't you take a seat and I'll grab you a drink."

She nods in agreement, sitting next to her mother. As I go

to get some punch I hear the clock chime midnight. All of a sudden I see Bella coming running through the ballroom toward the exit.

"That bastard. I'll kill him," I mumble, as I prepare to chase my sister to ensure she's okay.

"Bella stop!" I yell to her, out of breath. I finally reach her near the bottom of the steps outside the castle.

"Rodrick, I must go. The magic's almost spent. Please, I must go. I love you brother. But please let me go," Bella pleads with me.

Bella is in such a hurry she loses one of her shoes. I pick it up and call to her, but she has already taken off. I turn to go back to the party as Luke makes his way down the stairs toward me.

"Where has she gone? Do you know her? Why did you come out here?" Prince Luke is bombarding me with questions.

"No, I don't know who she is. I was making sure you didn't upset her since she was in such a rush to leave," I explain to him. " All she said was she couldn't be late. But she did leave this shoe."

I hand him the shoe and go back to my Cora Ann.

To be continued …

ACKNOWLEDGMENTS

First off, I would like to thank my mom for being my number one fan and supporter! And then my sisters Jenée and Kayleigh who, no matter how much we have fought, have always had my back! I would like to thank my husband Bill and son Spyder for letting me take the time out to write, and supporting me in this journey. And my old and new friends I have made on this journey of writing! With out any of you this book wouldn't be possible (Sosha, Jenée, Brandi, Crystal, Laura, Caitlyn, Jenn, & Jess) and all the awesome Indie authors and Indie community. Without you guys, this would not be possible.

And the biggest thanks of all is to Lacey for letting me be a part of this!

ABOUT THE AUTHOR

Kassie is new to the writing world. She's married with one crazy teenage son. (And three fat cats) She's always loved to write. Her twin sister writing a book
was the kick in the butt to get her to do it for herself. She
also loves reading traveling with family and friends,
Doctor Who, Supernatural, The Walking
Dead and cute cat videos.

YOU CAN FIND K.A MORSE HERE:

Bookbub:
www.bookbub.com/profile/k-a-morse
Instagram:
https://www.instagram.com/authork.a.morse/
Twitter:
@KA_Morse1
Amazon:
amazon.com/author/kamorse

FB Group:
https://www.facebook.com/groups/cursedreaders
FB Page:
www.facebook.com/kamorse1/

ALSO BY K.A. MORSE

Rylee's Awakening

Rylee's Reckoning

Loss of Eris (coming soon)

Operation Ann: Infected Crisis (coming soon)

Anthologies:

Melissa & The Lost Tomb of Akila

A Date With Death

Made in the USA
Columbia, SC
14 May 2019